I Heard the Owl Call My Name
by Margaret Craven

"A book thoughtful readers will surely return to again and again....It is hard to imagine a more complete and fulfilling book than this."
—*The Times Literary Supplement* (London)

"Moving, though not sentimental, the novel conveys well a vanishing way of life in a Northwest Pacific setting....Compelling." —*Library Journal*

"Appealing to all ages...a terrific job...the author draws heavily on the Indian lore of the Pacific Northwest."
—*Best Sellers*

"A moving statement of a conflict between two societies."
—*New Statesman*

"It will tug at your heartstrings." —*Hartford Courant*

"You'll love it...the book simply glows."
—*The News Journal* (Wilmington)

Also by Margaret Craven

**AGAIN CALLS THE OWL
WALK GENTLY THIS GOOD EARTH
THE HOME FRONT**

I HEARD THE OWL
CALL MY NAME

**MARGARET
CRAVEN**

This book is for the Tsawataineuk Tribe
at Kingcome Village, B.C.,
and for Eric Powell

A LAUREL BOOK
Published by
Dell Publishing
a division of
Bantam Doubleday Dell Publishing Group, Inc.
1540 Broadway
New York, New York 10036

The trademark Laurel® is registered in the U.S. Patent and Trademark Office and in other countries.

The trademark Dell® is registered in the U.S. Patent and Trademark Office.

ISBN: 0-440-34369-0

Reprinted by arrangement with Doubleday, a division of Bantam Doubleday Dell.

Printed in the United States of America

Published simultaneously in Canada

January 1980

60 59 58 57 56 55 54 53 52

RAD

CONTENTS

PART ONE

Yes, my lord-no, my lord

The doctor said to the Bishop, "So you see, my lord, your young ordinand can live no more than three years and doesn't know it. Will you tell him, and what will you do with him?"

The Bishop said to the doctor, "Yes, I'll tell him, but not yet. If I tell him now, he'll try too hard. How much time has he for an active life?"

"A little less than two years if he's lucky."

"So short a time to learn so much? It leaves me no choice. I shall send him to my hardest parish. I shall send him to Kingcome on patrol of the Indian villages."

"Then I hope you'll pray for him, my lord."

But the Bishop only answered gently that it was where he would wish to go if he were young again, and in the ordinand's place.

ONE

He stood at the wheel, watching the current stream, and the bald eagles fishing for herring that waited until the boat was almost upon them to lift, to drop the instant it had passed. The tops of the islands were wreathed in cloud, the sides fell steeply, and the firs that covered them grew so precisely to the high tide line that now, at slack, the upcoast of British Columbia showed its bones in a straight selvage of wet, dark rock.

"There's the sign of an old village," said the Indian boy who was his deckhand.

His eyes sought a beach from which, long ago, the big stones had been removed so that the war canoes could be pulled up stern first. But there was no beach. There was nothing but clean, straight selvage, and a scattered mound of something broken and white in the gray of rain against the green of spruce, and he remembered the words Caleb had quoted him, and he repeated them now.

" 'When you see clam shells, know it is Indian country. Leave it alone.' "

"Queen Victoria," the Indian boy said quickly. "Some people didn't hear her."

Caleb had prepared him for this one, the first he was to know: "He's been working for a year in a mill town and is eager to return to his village. You'll not take the boat out without him until you get your papers. He could handle a boat when he was ten, and he knows more about the coast than you will ever learn. You'll think he's shy, and you'll be wrong. When you shake his hand, you'll know at once it's a gesture he's learned which has no meaning. In his eyes you'll see a look that is in the eyes of all of them, and it will be your job to figure out what it means, and what you are going to do about it. And he will watch you—they will all watch you—and in his own time he will accept or reject you."

Caleb, the old canon, had come out of retirement to acquaint him with all the endearing—and exasperating—little ways of the forty-foot diesel launch upon which his life would depend.

Back up. Go forward. Up and down the straits. In and out the lower inlets in a mild chop, in a moderate chop, in a gale. The tide-book open by the compass because you came with the tide, you went with the tide, you waited for the tide, and sometimes you prayed for the tide. Check the oil pressure and the shaft bearings. Pump the bilge. Watch for the drift logs. Count the lights on the masts of the tug boats that showed the size of their booms.

Because Caleb was old, the young man had thought, of course, he would be garrulous and full of reminiscence, but he was wrong. The talk had been entirely nautical. Even in the galley, over meals which the young man cooked, Caleb had occasionally dropped what surely could not, yet must, be godly counsel.

"Be sure to use the Victorian 'we,' lad."

"When you bury anybody, remember to look in the box the very last minute. Forty years ago up at Fort Rupert I buried the wrong man, and even now the RCMP has not forgotten it."

"Don't call them cannibals. It was never true literally. No one alive has seen the famous dance

in which the young man, maddened by the cannibal spirit, returns to his village crying for flesh
and carrying a body taken from a grave tree."

Then one evening they had tied up at the marina of Powell River where the Indian boy had
been working, and Caleb lived.

"He'll be here early in the morning, and he'll
help you load the organ the local church is send-
ing to Kingcome Village. Don't be sorry for yourself because you are going to so remote a parish.
Be sorry for the Indians. You know nothing and
they must teach you," and Caleb had blessed him
and ambled off, bare-headed in the rain, a man
whose work on the coast was so legendary that it
was said the Archbishop of Canterbury greeted
him by his first name and a joke old between
them, "Tell me, Caleb, how's your trap line? Any
poaching?"

Then he was alone in the galley and sure of the
look he would see in the Indian's eyes. The tribes
of the villages which would form his patrol belonged to a people that had never been at war with
the white man. They lived where they had always
lived. They fished as they had always fished,
known for their intelligence and a culture that
was perhaps the most highly developed of any native band on the continent. In the old days when a
chief had given a great feast for his rivals, he let
the fire that burned in the center of his ceremonial
house catch the roof beams until the red hot em-
bers fell, knowing that until he gave the sign, no
guest dared move lest he admit the host's fire had
conquered him. When he served his guests from
the great ceremonial dishes, he spilt hot grease on
their bare arms to see if he could make them
wince. And sometimes he broke his own copper—big as a shield, its buying power as great as

three thousand of the white man's dollars—broke it to show to his guests his disdain for his own wealth. Surely the look would be one of arrogance.

In the morning he awakened early, dressed, put the coffee on to boil, and went up the ladder into the wheelhouse and out onto the deck. On the float waited the first one.

He waited patiently as if he had waited all his life, as if he were part of time itself. He was twenty-seven, perhaps, which was the age of the young vicar. He wore a fisherman's dark trousers and jacket; a pair of gum boots hung over one shoulder. Beside him were his belongings in a heavy cardboard box, tied with string.

The young vicar jumped down on the float.

"Welcome aboard. I'm Mark—Mark Brian," and he held out his hand.

"I'm Jim Wallace," the Indian said shyly, and he took the hand with no answering pressure.

There was pride in his eyes without arrogance. Behind the pride was a sadness so deep it seemed to stretch back into ancient mysteries Mark could not even imagine, and he felt that small thrill of fear, of anticipation, which a man knows if he's lucky enough to meet and recognize his challenge.

He led the way aboard. Eager to be off, the two of them worked hard, loading the organ onto the aft deck, covering it with a canvas, and lashing it tight.

Then they started north in a moderate swell and a driving rain, past the fishing village of Lund, past Cortes and Redonda, through the Yuculta Rapids, with Jim, the Indian, fighting the tide for the wheel. Just before dark they came to a lonely float in Shoal Bay.

"Shall we spend the night here?" Mark asked carefully. "Shall we have supper? I'll get it."

Now, on the second afternoon in the twentieth hour of passage, he stood at the wheel, approaching the first village which was to be part of his patrol.

"How soon now?"

"Very soon now. First you will see Ghost Island. It is where the Indians of Gilford village once buried their dead."

"In the ground?"

"No—in low sheds. Most of them have fallen and broken. If you go there now, you stumble over skulls green with moss."

He saw the small island, lovely as a jade jewel, and he slowed the boat and passed the village with its rare beach, white with clam shells, its stretch of cedar houses facing the water, and four great cedar posts standing in the rain—all that was left of some ancient ceremonial house.

"This is the same tribe as yours at Kingcome?"

"No, but we're close relatives. Each February we come here to clam. Once the Indian agent asked us to live here because he could step easily onto the big float without getting his feet wet."

"And you refused?"

"No. Our old people said, 'We are going to Hollywood,' and we came. We had some fine dancing, the air filled with duck down. We saw the famous blanket trimmed with a thousand eagle beaks, and because we are not permitted to buy liquor to serve in our own homes, the boys traded two masks for three cases of beer, and we drank it very fast and got very drunk."

"And then?"

"Then we returned to our own village."

Beyond the village, inches above the high tide

mark, Mark saw two carved killer whales, topped by a full moon.

"It's only the grave of Johnny Ray who was drowned," Jim told him. "When you come here to marry, to bury, to hold church in the school house, they will say to you, 'Johnny's hiding in the bush, and he steals things and scares our women. What'll we do?'"

In Cramer Pass a school of porpoise refused to move out of the boat's way, and watched the boat, heads up, headed straight for the boat and, at the last moment, leapt aside. And in the late afternoon they stopped to take on oil and water at the last point of contact with the outside world, a store where the loggers and Indians came for mail and supplies, built on a float, cabled to the steep island side.

The young vicar introduced himself to the oil agent and handed him a list of groceries he wished filled.

"Biggest order I'll fill this week. Newcomers don't buy here. They fill up south where things are cheaper."

"I know. Caleb told me," and the man's wife filled the order while he helped Jim with the oil. Two small raccoons, making a strange whirring sound, begged Mark for bread and took it gently in their strange little hands. When they were leaving, the wife of the oil agent gave Mark a bundle.

"One of your pals left his duds here," she said, "Caleb, probably," and Mark opened the bundle to find a cassock, its hem thick with dried mud.

Then they went on, the young vicar preparing supper in the galley, handing up plates of food and mugs of coffee. The Indian ate standing at the wheel; Mark perched on the high stool beside him.

No tug boat passed now; no huge boom of mixed logs. There was nothing but a lonely magnificence of sea and islands. When they went through Pamphrey's Pass and into Kingcome Inlet, which was the last, Mark saw the dorsal fin of a killer whale cruising slowly down the far side.

"Sometimes they rub against the boat," the Indian told him. "Sometimes they jump out of the water and come down flat with a terrific smash to knock off the barnacles that grow on the underside of their bodies."

"Why are we slowing?"

"Because we're passing the float house of Calamity Bill, the hand-logger. See his shack there and his A-frame? If we go too fast the wake of our boat will knock the nails out of his float, and he'll come out shaking his fist and swearing. He wears two sets of long-legged underwear and he changes one."

"The inside one, I hope."

"No—the outside one. The other's part of his skin, and when she knows you better, the wife of the oil agent at the float store will ask you to help her get it off him and into her washing machine."

"Oh, no, she won't."

They slipped through a pass so narrow Mark was sure the boat would scrape on a huge rock shaped like a whale and covered with brown seaweed.

"My people call it 'Whale Pass' because long ago the gods turned a whale into that rock."

Now they could see the great mountains lifting into the sky. On the far side of the inlet was a strip of bare granite, like the ragged scar of some huge grizzly, where a slide had peeled off every tree, every bit of soil. They could see the little falls that cascaded down cliffs, green with moss.

The young vicar said to himself, "If man were to vanish from this planet tomorrow, here he would leave no trace that he ever was."

They moved up the twenty-mile inlet with the dusk deepening into dark, the raindrops glistening, falling slowly in the searchlight, an occasional little fish darting through the white, spumy wake off the bow. And they came at last to the government float, a third of a mile from the inlet's end and three and one-half miles from the village of Kingcome. They tied up on the inside of the float where the boat would not roll.

"In the morning how will we manage?"

"In the morning we will lower the speed boat and I will go first with your gear and food. I will return with boys from the village and two of the thirty-foot canoes, and they will help load the organ and take it to the village."

"Up the river?"

"Yes. On the cliffs before you reach the river, you will see paintings of cattle, sheep, goats and coppers that mark the gifts given in a great tribal potlatch. There were so many that, put end to end, it is said they would have reached from the village three miles down the inlet."

"The paintings are very old?"

"Less than thirty years. The potlatch was in 1936."

In the cabin under the bow the young vicar awakened in the night. The rain had stopped. Through the open porthole he could hear the wind murmuring in the firs, and the distant mewing of the gulls.

Somewhere in the dark night beyond the inlet and up the river waited the village, and he lay still, remembering all the Bishop had told him of the village when he had first asked him to come:

"It is an old village—nobody knows how old. According to the myth, after the great flood two brothers were the only human beings left alive in the world, and they heard a voice speak and it said, 'Come, Wolf, lend them your skin that they may go fleetly and find themselves a home.' And in the wolf's skin the brothers moved south until they came to a small and lovely valley on a river's edge, surrounded by high mountains, and here they returned the skin to their friend, the wolf, and they threw a magic stone to see which one would build his village here, and Quelele, the younger, moved on, and Khawadelugha, the elder, built his house, and in his dances he moved right as even now the dancers move right because the wolf moved right, and on his totem he carved a wolf as one of the crests of his tribe.

"The Indian name of the village is Quee which means 'inside place,' and according to the tribal history its site was chosen wisely because the river, its access, is treacherous and easily defended. But the enemy was wise also, and in the great tribal wars it came through a mountain pass and down the river, and the spirit that lives in Whoop-Szo, the Noisy Mountain, that is across the river and towers over the village, heard the enemy coming and sent down a slide and buried it.

"Now Kingcome is known as a compact, Christian village, and this means that to run smoothly the elected chief, the vicar and the agent from the Indian Affairs Department must be co-operative and wise, and though I am sure the Lord could pass a small miracle and manage this, He seldom does. Once there was a chief who agreed with anyone on anything. Once there was an agent

who said there was no use educating the Indian
because if you did, you'd have to find him a job,
and he was bound to die off anyway. And once the
church sent a man to Kingcome who had never
worked out well anywhere because it was sure
here he could do no harm. All were wrong, and
the village survived them.

"The Indian knows his village and feels for his
village as no white man for his country, his town,
or even for his own bit of land. His village is not
the strip of land four miles long and three miles
wide that is his as long as the sun rises and the
moon sets. The myths are the village and the
winds and the rains. The river is the village, and
the black and white killer whales that herd the fish
to the end of the inlet the better to gobble them.
The village is the salmon who comes up the river
to spawn, the seal who follows the salmon and
bites off his head, the bluejay whose name is like
the sound he makes—'Kwiss-kwiss.' The village
is the talking bird, the owl, who calls the name of
the man who is going to die, and the silver-tipped
grizzly who ambles into the village, and the little
white speck that is the mountain goat on Whoop-
Szo.

"The fifty-foot totem by the church is the village, and the Cedar-man who stands at the bottom holding up the eagle, the wolf and the raven!
And a voice said to the great cedar tree in Bond
Sound, 'Come forth, Tzakamayi and be a man,'
and he came forth to be the Cedar-man, the first
man-god of the people and more powerful than
all others."

And the Bishop had been silent for a moment
before he added slowly, "This is the village. If you
go there, from the time you tie up at the float in

the inlet, the village is you. But there is one thing you must understand. They will not thank you. Even if you should leave a broken man, they will not thank you. There is no word for thank you in Kwákwala."

TWO

The next morning the young vicar and his Indian deckhand were up at daylight. After a hurried breakfast in the galley, they went up on deck and jumped down onto the float to survey the day.

The rain had stopped, the wind had softened, and the sky was blue, flecked with cloud.

They swung out and lowered the small boat, and they stowed in it the young vicar's gear and everything that was to go to the village except the organ. Then Jim put on his gum boots, undid the line, climbed into the boat and started the outboard motor, and he was off to the mouth of the river without a word.

While he was gone, the young vicar worked on the boat. Already he had begun to think of the boat as he thought of his own arms and legs, an extension of himself. Caleb had told him how frequently a fisherman lost a boat because he was too busy with the catch to check its bilge.

"There is no more beautiful sight than a boat burning in the night," Caleb had said dryly.

Mark went over the engine room slowly, double-checking everything. He washed the dishes in the galley, placing them carefully behind the little racks that held them tight in a gale. He checked the log, put away the charts, made up the berths, cleaned the refrigerator, and closed the portholes. When he was done, the sun was high in the sky, and he went out on deck to await the canoes.

He heard them coming far down the inlet, the

outboard motors sharp in the cedar air, and then he saw them, one black, one green, each thirty feet long, and narrow.

Jim had brought with him four young men of the village, and to Mark they looked strangely alike, with the same watchful, waiting eyes. Jim spoke to them in their own language, and when they had maneuvered the canoes to the stern of the boat, they lashed them together, while he and Mark untied the organ and removed the canvas that covered it.

Now it occurred to Mark that every single thing that went to Kingcome had to be taken up the river and for the first time he knew the stolid, stubborn indifference of the inanimate.

They moved the organ onto the gunwale of the aft deck. They tugged, pulled, shoved and lifted—the young vicar trying awkwardly to help, afraid the canoes would tip over and the organ end in the salt chuck. At last the organ was balanced on the canoes. Mark locked the boat, put on his gum boots, and took his place on the narrow crosspiece which was the seat, and they started up the inlet.

Even on this, one of the last good days of fall, it was cold, the water calm, and deep green from the shadow of the cedars. The falls slipped down the mossy cliffs. The mountains were snow-tipped above the timber line. When they passed the potlatch paintings and reached the muskeg near the mouth of the river, the hand of the Welcome totem rose above the trees, and hundreds of small birds, of ducks and geese, rose at their passing.

They entered the river, passed the snags and the log jam, slowing now to seek the channels, to avoid the sandbars where the water was shallow. And up the river on the left Mark saw Whoop-Szo, the Noisy Mountain, and the white barked alders that edged the bank, and flying over them the sleek black ravens. But on the right he saw only one thing, the little white church of Saint George.

The Indians took the canoes close to the shore and stepped out into the icy river. As carefully as they had placed the organ onto the canoes, they lifted it and carried it onto the black sands of Kingcome and up the little path that led past the old vicarage to the church.

They carried it up the steps to the porch, through the door, and set it down inside the church. Jim pulled over a bench, sat down and pedaled vigorously. Mark poked a key. Nothing happened.

"Oh, no!"

"It's a little damp. It will dry out in time."

Then Mark walked slowly down the center aisle toward the hand-carved altar and the great, carved, golden eagle which was the lectern, its talons close together, its head turned so that it looked most smugly down its beak, its wings slightly parted to hold the Bible. He saw the carved chair where the Bishop must sit when he came here, and the life-sized Indian painting of Christ holding a little lamb. His face was the Indian's face, His eyes the Indian's eyes, and in them the depth of sadness.

He turned away slowly; he was alone in the church. He walked down the aisle to the door and saw Jim waiting on the steps. No one else was visible, not even a child or a dog.

"Shall we go to the vicarage?" Jim asked.

They walked back to the old vicarage on the little path through the trees, and as they drew near, Mark heard a strange sound.

On the broken step of the vicarage sat an old

Indian woman, her face scratched and bleeding. She was wailing loudly.

"One of the professional mourners," Jim told him. "There are three. When somebody dies they take turns wailing day and night."

"I did not see her when we passed the vicarage carrying the organ to the church."

"She saw you, and was afraid. She hid."

"And why here? Why does she wail at the vicarage?"

"Because the bodies are kept in the vicarage until burial."

As they approached the steps the old Indian woman scuttled into the trees. Jim opened the door and they stepped inside. On boards laid across two trestles was a small body covered with a plastic sheet. Mark lifted the sheet and drew it back, and he looked at what lay under it, and put the sheet down carefully.

"Who is he?"

"The weesa-bedó—the little, small boy. He had a birth injury and did not grow like the others. He was sailing a paper boat at the river's edge and fell in. When they saw him floating on the water, the other children thought he was a doll."

"And why—why hasn't he been buried?"

"Because no burial permit has been given. The chief councillor went at once to the nearest radio-telephone and summoned the RCMP, but no one has come yet."

"Then we had better call again."

"The constable will come today. The old men say so."

"How do they know?"

"How did they know you were coming today? They almost always know. Besides it is the first good day and he will come soon now. It is a five hour trip from Alert Bay, and he will want to get back before night, and he will be young, and he will be hard."

"How do you know he will be young?"

"An older man would not wait ten days."

"Will you take me to the mother?"

But when they had walked up the path through the trees and up the steps of one of the little cedar houses, and knocked on the door and entered, Mark did not know what to say to the woman who waited.

She waited as if she had waited all her life, as if she were part of time itself, gently and patiently. Did she remember that in the old days the Indian mother of the Kwakiutl band who lost a child kicked the small body three times and said to it, "Do not look back. Do not turn your head. Walk straight on. You are going to the land of the owl"?

He took her hands and spoke to her. "The old men say the constable will come soon. Then we shall bury him, and you can rest," but in her soft dark eyes he found no response at all. When he returned to the vicarage to wait, he saw Jim and an older Indian, no doubt the chief councillor, walk down the path to the river, and he heard the motor of a speed boat, and watched it come and stop close to the beach.

The RCMP officer was young, and it was obvious why he had been long in coming. He had been waiting for a fair day, because with him he had brought his girl. He picked her up and carried her to the sands and Mark was sure he knew the words he spoke to her. "Look around as much as you want. Don't go into any of the houses except the church. This won't take long."

Then the RCMP officer talked to the chief councillor, both voices loud and angry.

"You had no business to move him. You know the rules. In an accident the body must not be moved."

"We were not sure he was dead. We thought we could revive him."

"And when you couldn't, you should have covered him and left him there."

"On the edge of the river with the tide coming in? In the rain?"

"Where is the body now?"

"It is in the vicarage."

They came toward Mark, followed by several Indian men.

"I'm Constable Pearson. Who are you?"

"Mark Brian. I am the new vicar-in-residence."

"And what do you know of this?"

"Nothing. I have just arrived."

"Let's go in. I'll want an autopsy."

"I'm afraid it is a little late for that."

They entered the vicarage, Constable Pearson plucked the sheet from the small body and leaned toward it. Then he bolted from the room, down the rickety steps, and into the bush where he was very sick. The Indians were delighted. Laughter rose in their eyes, higher and higher, filling them, and hovering there in tremulous balance. Not a drop overflowed. When Constable Pearson emerged from the bush, all the eyes were sad again, and all the faces solemn.

"May I offer you a cup of tea?" asked the young vicar, his voice excessively polite. "I notice there is smoke coming from the chimneys of several of the houses. I think we could manage a cup of tea."

Constable Pearson did not wish a cup of tea. He wanted to give the burial permit and leave. The forms must be filled out. Was there a table somewhere? Mark led him to the church, and on the top of the organ that wouldn't play they made out the forms, and the constable left.

"Now," said Jim, "we can hold the service for the boy."

"In the church?"

"No—in the open air. We have a new burial ground, but it is a mile from the village, and each time anyone dies the path must be cleared. The chief wishes the weesa-bedó to be buried in the old burial ground just beyond the end of the village, and the box is made, and the grave is dug, and already my people are gathering there."

"I'll get my things."

"I'll help you," and they scrambled through Mark's gear that had been piled on the porch of the vicarage until they found a cassock and his Book of Common Prayer.

Then for the first time Mark walked the main path from one end of the village to the other, past the cedar houses that faced the path, the ceremonial house, the battered eagle poised on a slender shaft. One totem pole was so old he could discern only the top figure, a bear wearing at a most jaunty angle the lid of a garbage can to keep him from weathering further.

Beyond the village they entered the deep woods, Jim walking quickly, Mark holding his cassock out of the mud, and trying not to slip off the small saplings that made a bridge across one swampy place where the trees were so thick the sun never penetrated. At last they came into a glade and stopped, and stared.

"It is only the grave trees. In the old days each family had its own trees. The lower limbs were cut off as protection against the animals, and the boxes were hoisted by ropes and tied one above another in the tops. Many have fallen as you can see, and the grave sheds that were built later have fallen and most of the old carvings."

Later Mark could never remember the details of his first burial. Only parts remained clear. The faces of the tribe, which all looked alike, lifted and waiting in the brooding woods.

But the words were the same simple words that have been said for the weesa-bedós of all men, and it was as if they had been written for this place and this time. When he spoke, "I will lift up mine eyes unto the hills," there were the mountains rising above the great trees, and when he read that small and lovely prayer, " . . . protect him all day long until the shadows lengthen and the evening comes . . . ," the sun had slipped beneath the mountain tops, and the shadows were lengthening on the small grave at his feet. When it was done, he managed to find among all the faces the mother, and this time it was she who touched his sleeve gently and thanked him with her eyes.

But the tribe did not disperse, and he sensed there was something yet unfinished of which he had no part, and he said, "I will go back to the village now, Jim."

"I'll go with you."

On the way back Mark could hear an old man's voice speaking loudly in the burial glade, almost shouting.

"It is the eldest. He is speaking the ancient Elizabethan Kwákwala which the young no longer know. Where there is no written language, anything which must be remembered must be said."

When they reached the vicarage, the trestle was gone. Someone had made a fire in the old food stove and let the vicarage fill with the smoke of green cedar and let the breeze clear it. Two places were set on the tattered oilcloth of the kitchen table, a plate and a fork, and in the center of the table was a board holding an unappetizing mess of something black and steaming.

"We have had nothing to eat since breakfast. Shall we have dinner?" Jim asked. "It is probably old Marta who brought it."

"What is it?"

"Seaweed and corn. It is called gluckaston. Try it. You'll like it," and the young vicar tried it and found it excellent.

"I will not need you tomorrow. I'll be busy here in the vicarage."

"Then I'll go fishing. Maybe I'll get drunk. Do you want to know why I'll get drunk?

"Because the weesa-bedó was my relative. When I was five, which was his age, my uncle gave a feast for me and I was given my third name and I danced. I had practiced the steps in play."

After the meal Jim helped carry the gear into the vicarage, and when he left, Mark walked with him onto the porch and watched him go up the path into the dark trees. Then he went inside by himself, into the sweet and spicy smell of death.

THREE

When dark came to the village there was a gentle, cautious confabulation about the young vicar who had come from the great outside world. The young women found an imminent need to exchange crochet patterns, and they met like a huddle of young hens and whispered about his looks, his manners, even his clean fingernails.

Chief Eddy, on his way to the social hall, met Jim on the path and he asked, "How does he seem to you?"

"He will be no good at hunting or fishing. He knows little of boats. All the time he says we. 'Shall we have dinner now? Shall we tie up here?' Pretty soon he will say, 'Shall we build a new vicarage?' He will say we and he will mean us," and they both smiled.

In the social hall Chief Eddy found the old men waiting to play the ancient guessing game of Lahell, the benches in place, the bones on the floor. He sat down and the game began, all the players waiting for T. P. Wallace, the elder, the orator of the tribe, to mention the young vicar first.

T. P. was the only one alive now whose broad brow showed that as an infant it had been tightly bound with cedar bands. In his white shirt, tie and best jacket, he was as impressive as any Montreal executive, and cast in bronze his head would not have been out of place in that museum room reserved for the busts of the ancient Romans. He was slow to speak.

"Did you notice that at the graveside he left quietly and asked no questions?" They all nodded. "He respected our customs. And what will he say when he knows we are losing our sons, and that our young no longer understand the meaning of the totems?"

"When the constable was sick in the bushes," said Chief Eddy, "how well he held his laughter."

In one of the best houses of the village Mrs. Hudson, the matriarch, was pleased that a vicar was again in residence. The Bishop would surely come more frequently, perhaps even with a boatload of landlubber clergy to be fed and housed, and the young wives would gather here in her house to defer to her judgment, speaking softly in Kwákwala.

"What meat shall we have?"

"Roast beef." Or salmon. Or wild goose. Or duck.

"And what vegetable shall we have?" Mrs. Hudson's answer was always the same, and her small revenge on the white man, the intruder.

"Mashed turnips." No white man liked mashed turnips.

In a small neat house off the main path, Marta Stephens prepared to knit a toque to keep the new vicar's head warm when he came up the river in the winter. Marta was one of the grandmothers of the tribe. Her hair was white, which, in an Indian, means she was very old. Her face was finely wrinkled and of obvious gentility. She was the daughter of an hereditary chief, the wife of a chief, the mother of a chief. At the tribal feasts held for the Bishop, it was she who always slipped him a little dish of peas from her garden because he detested mashed turnips, and when he had first come to the village years before, cowering in a canoe under a tarpaulin in a heavy rain, it had been she who held a cup of coffee to his lips because his hands were so cold he could not hold it.

"And how did you like our river?" And the Bishop had answered dryly that getting into heaven could be no harder than reaching this village, and didn't Mrs. Stephens agree it was bound to be warmer?

In the poorest house Sam, the unlucky one, considered how best to approach the new vicar for a loan. Soon, of course, while he was green and before the Bishop had a chance to warn him. Sam was descended from slaves and in the old days to be a slave was to be worse than a nothing. He had no pride. His boats burned under him. When he reached the fishing grounds, the fish had not come yet, or they had seen him and fled. Sam wanted only two things in life, liquor and sex, and when he had no money for liquor, he beat his wife and Ellie, his daughter.

In the night Jim awakened and asked himself, "Will he know that here I am free?"

In the night Keetah, Mrs. Hudson's granddaughter, awakened also, the only one of the tribe who had no English proper name, and she asked herself, "Will he know that my Gordon feels himself trapped here?"

In the night in the last house next to the old burial ground old Peter, the carver, heard a flight of wild geese pass over the village, honking loudly, and he counted the seconds of their passage as was his custom. But it was not a huge migration. No more than a mile long. "How long will he be here before he knows that I live among the dead?"

In the teacher's house the only other white man in the village did not think of the vicar at all. He didn't even know he had arrived; he didn't even know he was coming. This was the teacher's second year in the village. He did not like the Indians and they did not like him. When he had returned from his summer holiday, a seaplane had deposited him at flood tide under the alders on the far side of the river, and he had stood there in the rain yelling loudly, "Come and get me," and T. P. had announced, "If he cannot be more polite, let him stay there." It was old Marta who finally poled across the river and plucked him from the bank. The teacher had come to the village solely for the isolation pay which would permit him a year in Greece studying the civilization he adored.

At star-fall a young buck walked through the village to drink at the river. He was unafraid of guns. The Indian hunted for food, not for fun, and when he found it necessary to kill a deer, he did not shoot him. If possible, he knocked him over the head with a club.

Just before dawn when day and night were locked in their tug-of-war, and day began slowly to push away the dark, Ellie, the little lost one, returned to the house of Sam, her father. Ellie went willingly to the bed of any man who beckoned her, and since, at thirteen years, brutality was all she knew of masculine attention, she liked best the man who mistreated her the most.

FOUR

In the morning when the young vicar stepped onto the rickety porch, it was as if the funeral of the weesa-bedó had never happened. The village was quiet, and utterly at peace. In the river he could see a long, black canoe moored, and as he watched, an older Indian woman waded out into the icy water, climbed into the canoe, poled into the center of the stream and dumped her garbage, and he knew that was what he would do—in the sun, in the sleet, in the rain, and the snow.

When he tried to start a fire in the kitchen stove, the wood was wet and the stovepipe smoked, and when he went to open a can of coffee, there was no can opener, and he finally extracted sufficient coffee for two cups by hammering a hole in the top of the can with a nail. For the first time it occurred to him that just to stay alive, fed, and clean here was going to occupy many hours a day.

After breakfast, he went to the church, and for the first time noticed that the tower was broken, that there were no altar hangings and no candles. When he approached the altar, he saw that the frontal piece—no doubt given by some small town church that had acquired a new one—was propped up on old crates. And, more important, on this fine day of early fall, the little church was dank and cold. He knew that unless he wanted to stand by the golden eagle on a winter Sunday and watch his congregation freeze between the "dearly beloved brethren" and the blessing, he must manage somehow to nail plywood over the bare studding and insulation behind it. He knew also that even if he managed it, he would be up at dawn every Sunday hurrying along the little path from the vicarage, a coat hastily flung over his pajamas, on his way to rattle up a fire in the big, round, black stove.

Then he returned to the vicarage and went over it carefully—all two rooms of it. There was no plumbing. The paper hung in shreds from the walls. The walls were discoloured and warped where the rain had entered. When he tried to open a window, the whole sill came loose in his hand, and the floor sagged under him. There was no doubt about it. The vicarage was falling down.

He had come to give and he was going to begin where every man is apt to begin who is sent to hold some lonely outpost. He was going to begin by begging. "I want this. I need that. I need paint. I need plywood. I would appreciate a couple of hundred pounds of insulation, and if it isn't too much trouble, send me a new vicarage complete with plumbing."

It was all wrong and he knew it. In desperation he shot an arrow prayer into the air: "Oh, dear Lord, what am I going to do about this vicarage?" He sent it aloft at ten in the morning and the Lord answered him promptly at twelve. Chief Eddy came to the door with a letter from the Bishop which had been brought in the mail bag by one of the fishermen some days previously, and forgotten in the confusion of yesterday's funeral.

The young vicar sat down at the kitchen table and opened it slowly. He knew it must have been written before he and Jim had started north, and he was afraid to read it.

"I am sure," wrote the Bishop, "that when you receive this, you will be aware that the old vicarage must be replaced. When you are ready, I shall make arrangements to have a pre-fabricated two-bedroom house delivered at the float at the end of the inlet. I can, of course, send no one to help you put it up. You must begin by working with your hands. The Indians work with their hands. This is the way they will respect you and this is your ministry."

Mark read it twice and had a sudden and appalling vision of hundreds of boards, kegs of nails, bolts and shingles, perhaps even a bathtub, all heavy, stubborn and totally inanimate, piled high on the float, waiting to be carried up the river by canoe.

He scurried through his luggage for paper and pencil, and he seated himself at the kitchen table and wrote to the Bishop.

"Please, my lord, do not send me a vicarage. At least, not yet. I do not even know how to get it up the river, much less put it up. I am going to begin today by cleaning the church. When I finish, I shall patch up the vicarage. It's strange, but since receiving your letter, I do not seem to find the sweet smell of death too oppressive."

He sealed the letter and gave it to Chief Eddy to go out by the first boat. Then he returned to the church, and in the tiny vestry in back he found an ancient broom, and he swept the church carefully. He made a fire in the big round stove and heated water. Then he scrubbed the strip of red linoleum that covered the center aisle.

"There is a bear loose in the church," said Mrs. Hudson, the matriarch, to T. P., the elder. "What a clatter he is making!"

"By evening he will be quieter," T. P. told her.

"By evening the bear will have blistered both paws."

The Indians were polite. They were not unfriendly. When he had cleaned the church, he worked on the vicarage with the broom and the scrub brush, and when he wearied and ambled to the river's edge where the women were smoking and drying fish, they smiled at him shyly. When he stopped in the door of the ceremonial house and looked beyond the dirt floor to the carved posts and the two-headed serpent painted on the rear wall, old Peter, the carver, who was working on a canoe, answered his questions.

"How are you going to widen it?" the vicar asked, and Peter told him he was going to fill the canoe with water and drop into it hot rocks to make the wood expand to the cedar stretchers, and when this was done, he would singe the bottom.

They were polite and this was all. When Jim returned from fishing, they went again down the river to the float and by the boat to the other villages which were part of his patrol, and in each he arranged to hold church in a schoolhouse or a private home once a month. It was always the same. The sad eyes. The shy smiles. The cautious waiting.

But for what? How must he prove himself? What was it they wished to know of him? And what did he know of himself here where loneliness was an unavoidable element of life, and a man must rely solely on himself?

On the river on the way back to Kingcome in the little speed boat, the young vicar knew that the Indians belonged here as the birds and fish belonged, that they were as much a part of the land as the mountains themselves. He was a guest in their house, and he knew, also, that this might never change, and he told himself what does it matter if a man is lonely? One does not die of it.

When they reached the village, he hoed out the wild grass that had grown rank around the vicarage. When this was done, he visited the sick. On his way back to the vicarage, he passed a small, weathered cedar house, its owner out in the yard trying to start an ancient washing machine hitched up to a small gasoline engine, and he stopped to help him.

The next morning he removed the broken board of the vicarage steps and the Indian he had helped came by to offer him a saw and found him a board for a new step.

In the afternoon he climbed up on the roof to see if he could stop the leaks, and Chief Eddy walked by to watch him.

"Aren't you afraid you'll fall through?" And Mark answered that he considered it not only possible, but likely.

"I'd rather come down on top of the vicarage than have the vicarage come down on me," and for a moment he saw humour rise in the sad eyes and hold.

He did not mention the Bishop's offer to send him a new vicarage. He had made up his mind that he would not ask help in getting it up the river, or putting it up. He would wait until they offered help, or do without it.

Sam, the ne'er-do-well, came over to watch him work, shedding large tears and shamelessly begging money, and Mark turned him down.

Also, the teacher accosted him on the path, asking that he intervene with the authorities that he be given proper supplies. Even the smallest villages were given more pencils and pads. Also, he was expected to pay for the paper tissues which he dropped so generously for the sniffling noses of his pupils. Furthermore, his house had no electricity, and its tiny bathroom was so small that when he sat upon the throne-of-thought he could not shut the door without hitting his knees, which was an outrage.

The young vicar suggested the teacher cut two round holes for his knees to stick through, and offered to trade his outhouse for the teacher's bathroom, but the teacher was not amused. There was one more thing he felt it his duty to inform the vicar. The vicar might as well know right now that as for himself, he was an atheist; he considered Christianity a calamity. He believed that any man who professed it must be incredibly naïve.

The young vicar grinned and agreed. There were two kinds of *naïveté*, he said, quoting Schweitzer; one not even aware of the problems, and another which has knocked on all the doors of knowledge and knows man can explain little, and is still willing to follow his convictions into the unknown. "This takes courage," he said, and he thanked the teacher and returned to the vicarage.

When he closed the door, he sensed he was not alone, and when he turned slowly, he welcomed his first visitors.

They were six years old perhaps—a little girl and boy. They had entered without knocking— never would he be able to teach them to knock— and they stood like fawns—too small to be afraid. They stood absolutely still, and they smiled, slowly and gently. When he asked their names, they did not answer, watching him from their soft, dark, sad eyes, as their ancestors must have watched the first white man in the days of innocence.

"I think," he said, "I shall go for a little walk,"
and the little boy said, "We will go with you."
When they went out the door, the boy ran ahead
to the grease pole that stood in front of the
church, and up it, hand over hand.

Mark held out his hand, and the little girl took
it, and they stood a moment, staring up at Whoop-
Szo, the Noisy Mountain, towering beyond the
river, and she said, as if it were very important,
"I love the snow on the mountains."

Thus, the children were his first friends, and for
love of their laughter he always kept his door
ajar. One day, when Chief Eddy stopped to see if
he had fallen yet through the roof of the vicarage,
the young vicar stopped his patching and descended the ladder.

"Chief Eddy," he said earnestly, "there is something I have been meaning to ask you. How do
you pronounce the name of your tribe?" It is
spelled Tsawataineuk.

"Jowedaino."

There was a silence.

"Would you mind saying it again?"

"Jowedaino," and Mark listened more carefully
than he had ever listened to any word in his entire life and could not tell if the word was
Zowodaino or Chowudaino.

"And the name of the band to which your tribe
belongs?" which in the books of anthropology is
written Kwakiutl.

"Kwacutal," and Mark listened and could not
tell if the word was Kwagootle, Kwakeetal or
Kwakweetul.

"And the name of the cannibal who lived at the
north end of the world?"

"Bakbakwalanuksiwae," and it came from the
chief's lips like a ripple.

"What chance did he have with a name like that? And what chance have I? I shall never be able to spell or pronounce even the name of this tribe."

"I can't spell it myself," said the chief. "Begin with something easier. Try saying how do you do. Weeksas—weeksas."

After that when Mark passed the Indians on the path, he said, "Weaksauce," exactly as the chief had said it, and saw the humour take their eyes.

On the first Sunday morning he tolled the church bell half an hour before the service. He was sure no one would come. He stayed in the tiny vestry behind the altar and waited.

He was wrong. Everyone came except the teacher, Sam, the sick and the very young. On the very first hymn he found he must never for an instant let go of a high note because if he did, his congregation would sink an octave and never come up again. He was young enough to be a little proud of his first sermon, to which he had given considerable thought: "It is better to be a small shrimp in the sea of faith than a dead whale on the beach."

When the service was over, he stood at the door, trying desperately to learn what the Indians called their English nicknames and to affix each to the right face. Marta Stephens was last, and it was now she presented the toque.

"To keep your head warm on the river," she explained, and the young vicar thanked her, and put it on.

"How do I look?"

"Like an egg. Exactly like an egg."

He walked down the steps with her, sensing somehow that she was to mean much to him.

"Mrs. Stephens, tell me something. Do you remember the first man who came here for the church?"

"Yes. He had a long white beard. He had to learn our language so he could teach us his. He said, 'What is this? What is that?' and sometimes we told him the wrong word to tease him. I am ashamed of it now. He was so patient. He was patient even with the children who pulled his beard."

"How do you know?"

"Because," Marta said, "I was one of them."

FIVE

Often in the first weeks, Mark was beset by a sense of futility, and always he was lonely. On the patrol to the other villages, which somehow he must bind together into a parish, hour passed hour and neither he nor Jim spoke a word. He gave up trying to know Jim, even hoping to understand him, and learned to wait, clinging staunchly to Caleb's Victorian we. In his turn Jim served him well and dutifully, the cautious waiting still in his eyes.

Then one late afternoon there was a change. They had been to the float store to pick up a load of plywood to cover the bare studdings in the church, and when they reached the government float at the end of the inlet, they left the load to bring up the river by canoe the next day, and started for the village in the speed boat. When they neared the river mouth on a rising tide, Jim stopped the engine and motioned Mark to be still.

They sat quietly, the boat drifting slowly, Jim watching a ripple line on the clear and sunless water. Then they saw it. A run of humpback salmon was entering the river to spawn in the Clearwater. Two or three feet beneath the surface Mark could see hundreds of silvery fish, pressed tight, moving secretly, almost stealthily, with a kind of desperate urgency, as an army moves to hold an outpost which must be reached at any cost. He watched, fascinated, until they had passed, and for a moment he was not sure that it had happened at all.

" 'Come, swimmer,' " he said. " 'I am glad to be alive now that you have come to this good place where we can play together. Take this sweet food. Hold it tight, younger brother.' "

Then, for the first time, the watchful waiting left the Indian's eyes and he said eagerly, "How did you know that? Where did you hear it?"

"It's a prayer your people once said to the salmon, and I read it in a book written long ago. The hook was called 'younger brother.' The halibut was called 'old woman.' When your people pulled a halibut into a canoe, they said, 'Go, old flabby mouth, and tell your uncles, and your cousins, and your aunts how lucky you were to come here.' But they spoke with respect of the salmon and they called him 'swimmer.' "

"The salmon is still the swimmer in our language, and I can remember my grandfather speaking to him as you do now. I had forgotten."

"Do you see him enter the river often?"

"No, not often. He enters usually at night."

"And in the end, does he always die?"

"Always. Both the males and the females die. On the way up the river the swimmer will pass the fingerlings of his kind coming down to the sea. They want to go and are afraid to go. They still swim upstream, but gently, letting the river carry them downstream tail first, and the birds and the larger fish prey upon them to devour them, and pretty soon they turn to face their dangers."

"And when they reach the open sea?"

"Then they are free. Nobody knows how far they go or where. When the time comes to return, their bodies tell them, and those hatched in the same stream separate from all the others and

come home together. And in the end the swimmer
dies, and the river takes him downstream, tail first,
as he started."

"Could we see the end?"

"Easily."

On one of the last lovely days of September
Mark packed a lunch and he and Jim went upriver in one of the smaller outboard canoes to
seek the end of the swimmer. Above the village
where the river curved left into rapids, they
stopped at a pool at the foot of Che-kwa-lá, the
falls, on a stream that fell into the river. Here it
was cool and misty, the spruce and the hemlock
hanging with moss, one huge cottonwood standing
guard. They stood for a long time watching the
troubled restless water of the falls coming to rest
in the deep quiet pool, and neither spoke.

Then they went on up the rapids of the river,
and a bear, fishing for the swimmer, saw them
come and scrambled into the trees, and the two
deer that had come to the river to drink saw
them also, and were gone in one lovely fluid
leap.

Well up the river they passed cedar shake cabins, smoke coming from the holes in their roofs,
and Mark could see some of the children of the
tribe playing under the trees.

"They have come to smoke fish," Jim told him.
"Each fall, families come to do this. It is a time
everyone likes. The children run wild and the
women talk. And at night the men sit by the fire
and tell the old myths, and when they return,
they are as well smoked as the fish."

When they came to the Clearwater where the
swimmer spawned, they turned off the motor and
paddled through deep quiet pools, overhung with
thick brush, to the little falls at the end of the

stream and pulled the canoe upon a small, rocky
beach of a little island, and they saw they were
not alone. Old Marta was there and the girl called
Keetah, and the two small children who were his
friends, come from the shake cabins to pick blueberries.

At lunch, which they shared, Mark felt at ease
for the first time. It was a picnic like any picnic.
The day was fair on the small and lovely island.
The children played as all children play, and the
girl called Keetah, in the faded blue denim slacks
and jacket, was a pretty girl anywhere.

"Mark wants to see the end of the swimmer,"
Jim announced after lunch, and Marta smiled
and said she was too old to hang over the pool's
edge flat on her middle; she would stay with the
children and pick the rest of the blueberries. Jim
found a place where an old maple grew over the
stream and the underbrush cast deep shadows.
There the three of them crept carefully to the
stream's edge and looked down.

Under the clear water they saw the female
swimmer digging the seed beds with her torn tail,
her sides deep red and blue, her fins battered and
worn.

"When she has laid her eggs and the waiting
males have covered them with milt, she will lin-
ger, guarding them for several days," Jim said.
"Let's try another pool." They moved again and
saw the end of the swimmer. They watched her
last valiant fight for life, her struggle to right herself when the gentle stream turned her, and they
watched the water force open her gills and draw
her slowly downstream, tail first, as she had started to the sea as a fingerling. Then they crept
away from the pool's edge and returned to Marta,

and Mark saw that in Keetah's eyes there were tears.

"It is always the same," she said. "The end of the swimmer is sad."

"But, Keetah, it isn't. The whole life of the swimmer is one of courage and adventure. All of it builds to the climax and the end. When the swimmer dies he has spent himself completely for the end for which he was made, and this is not sadness. It is triumph."

"Mark is right, Keetah," Marta said. "It is not sad. It is natural. When I was a child and a sea-hunter died, we believed he went to the land of the killer whale, and a land-hunter to the home of the wolves, and a slave to the home of the owls. But when twins were born in the village, we did not think they were children at all. They were swimmers."

"I have a twin sister," Mark said. "She is my only close relative," and they all laughed, and Marta said, "The swimmer is your relative. You belong to the salmon people."

On the way back to the village Mark and Jim spoke little. When they had moored the canoe, waded ashore, and were walking up the path to the vicarage, Mark said slowly, "Keetah is a beautiful girl. Do you not think so?"

"Yes. When she was at the government school in Alert Bay she was called the 'little princess.' She was homesick. When the children stood in line to receive the cod-liver oil, she went to the end of the line for another dosage because the oil tastes like the gleena in which we dip our food."

"She is married?"

"No—she is to marry Gordon. Her grandmother has arranged it. He is at the government school in

Alert Bay. He is older than the others there because he stayed out of school to help his uncle
with the fishing. But she will not marry him. She
will marry me."

"What makes you so sure?"

"Because I am the only other man in the village
she can marry. She is too closely related to the
others. She will marry me, keep my house, and
have my children, and I will leave her and go off
to fish."

"She does not like Gordon?"

"She likes him."

"Then what is the matter with him?"

"Gordon is Che-kwa-lá, which means fast moving water," Jim said slowly, "and Keetah is the
pool."

Whenever they came up the river from the
float, Mark watched for the swimmer, the pressed
silver forms moving secretly beneath the surface.
He did not see him again.

SIX

In late October the fishing days grew fewer, lessening slowly to an end. Now there were more men in the village. Sometimes Mark would see one setting off into the woods to hunt, his rifle held so easily it seemed part of the man himself. And sometimes he saw two starting off together, one man's arm over the shoulder of the other, and he knew this was no indication of homosexuality; it was the warrior-to-warrior relationship, centuries old. But never did he see groups of men talking loudly of the hunt that was planned, and this also was rooted in the past. If a man said aloud, "I will pursue the deer here; I will seek the bear there," some woman would hear him, and ten minutes later all the wives of the tribe would be promising each other venison and bear steaks, and discussing how to cook them, and the spirits that lived in the bear and the deer would hear them, and the game would hide.

One day in the vicarage over lunch, Mark questioned Jim about the hunting, and Jim asked if he'd like to go along, and Mark said he would—to watch, that is, since he was no hunter himself and had never shot anything larger than a rabbit or a duck.

"Have you had sufficient sustenance to suffice?" he asked when the meal was done, and Jim said, "What is this word *suffice*?" and Mark told him it meant "Have you had enough to eat?"

Early one morning, they went again upriver

with three other men from the village, and after
an hour on a mountain called Quanade, they followed a bear. However hard Mark tried to keep
up, he was always last, breaking through the underbrush with a frightful clatter, snagged on the
devil's club, slipping on the shale. When he was
sure he could not take another step, one of the Indians whirled and a shot sounded, and a large
brown form dropped. They approached it carefully.

"I thought we were following the bear," Mark
said to Jim.

"We were until he circled. He's been following
us for an hour."

"But there's no bullet hole."

"It is hidden by the fur and the rolls of fat," and
Mark saw the laughter rise and hold in all the
dark eyes.

"This bear did not die of a bullet," one of the
Indians told him gravely. "He died of shock. It's
the first time he's ever seen a vicar so far up on
the mountain."

In mid-afternoon one of the men shot a gray
timber wolf that weighed at least a hundred and
thirty pounds, its big mouth full of what seemed
to Mark an over-abundance of very large teeth,
and he and Jim took leave of the others and
walked through the woods back to the shake cabins to start supper and prepare the bough beds
upon which the blankets would be spread.

They trudged in silence for at least an hour.

"You know something, Jim?"

"What?"

"I think we're being followed."

"It's only the mate of the wolf that was killed.
When we move, she moves. When we stop, she
stops. Let's rest."

They rested, and Mark got out his pipe, filled, tamped and lighted it, trying very hard not to look back, trying not to show by squirming that he wished to go on. Finally Jim spoke. He spoke slowly and carefully.

"Have we had sufficient to suffice? Have we had enough?"

"Did you say we?"

"Yes."

"I don't know about you, but I have," and they went on quickly, leaving behind them the widow wolf and Caleb's splendid Victorian we that had served Mark well and that he would not use again.

That night, in the largest of the shake cabins, they lay close together on their bough beds in their clothes and their wool caps, the fire burning on the dirt floor, and the Indians talked so long of the man-god who lived in the sea and controlled the fishes that Mark went to sleep before he ever learned what the killer whale said to the swimmer, and the swimmer to the halibut. When he awoke the shake cabin was filled with smoke, his face was grimy with soot, his eyes stung, the bough bed had grown hard, and even with his head under the blankets, he could not stop coughing. He pulled on his boots—the only thing he'd taken off—and, plucking the top blanket, he crept for the door and out. He put the blanket around his shoulder and his back against a big cedar, and stood in the cool dark. Presently Jim joined him.

"What are you doing here? We thought we'd lost you."

"I couldn't stop coughing. I was afraid I'd awaken the others. Jim, don't ask me to creep behind a deer and wham him over the head with a club."

"I won't."

"And I'll never fish as well as the Indians. Sometimes I'm not even sure I'll learn to handle the boat."

"You are doing well with the boat. In another six months you will be almost as good as an Indian boy by the time he is ten."

They stood under the cedar in the rain until daybreak. Both knew there was friendship between them now, forged without words and needing none.

In November the rain fell in a slow and patient drizzle. Already the rain had become an element of life like the air Mark breathed, and when it stopped, he missed it somehow, and found himself listening for the drip, drip, drip that seemed now a necessary and comforting component of his life.

SEVEN

In November the hospital ship of the tiny Anglican fleet tied up at the float as it did every six weeks, and the doctor was brought up the river by canoe, and turned the old vicarage into a clinic. The doctor was new on the ship and had never pulled a tooth in his life. He could not hypnotize the Indians during the process as had his predecessor. When he did not wait long enough for the novocaine to take hold, Sam, his first patient, let out such horrific moans that little Ethel, one of the two children who had come first to the vicarage, hid in the woods. When the doctor had gone, Mark found her among the trees, and he took her to the vicarage, sat her in a chair, tied one end of a string around her wobbly baby tooth and the other to a doorknob, and he said, "Now, Ethel, I'll count ten, and then I'll kick the door shut."

"One-two-three," he counted, and he slammed the door on five and out flew the tooth.

"Nothing to it," he said, and while he picked up the swabs, the lint, and the bandages, little Ethel swept up the teeth from the vicarage floor.

A week later one of the boys of the village was very ill in the night with what Mark was sure was acute appendicitis. The hospital ship was in Seymour Inlet, too far to come quickly, and a bush plane, if he could manage to summon one by the radio-telephone on the boat, could not land on the river at night. He and Jim placed the boy in blankets, took him by canoe to the boat, packed his side in crushed ice and took him to Alert Bay.

When they had delivered the patient safely to the hospital and started back to the village, they found the straits shrouded in a thick fog, and the boat rolling heavily in the swell that came down Queen Charlotte Sound. But Jim knew the way, sounding the whistle to catch an echo from an island or an inlet side. They crept up the inlet to the float, and they crept up the river past the log jams and the snags, the water gurgling around them, Mark, who had forgotten his Kingcome slippers, trying to hold his feet out of the rain water in the bottom of the canoe.

When they reached the vicarage, Marta had started a fire, and set a pot of soup on the back of the stove and a loaf of homemade bread on the table, and they ate ravenously.

With December all the things in the village— the stubborn, inanimate things—revolted at once. The church stove smoked. The wet wood refused to burn. The hot water boiler in the house of Chief Eddy burst its seams. The mended roof of the old vicarage developed sundry leaks, the rain hitting the waiting buckets with a rhythmic plop. The boat developed gasket trouble, and the generator that operated the lights in the church—the only one in the village—refused to start fifteen minutes before the Sunday Evensong. Mark took off his surplice, put on his heavy Indian sweater. Out came the wrenches, off came the fuel line. He drained the fuel tank. He bled the air from the fuel line, then connected it all up again. He cranked, talking steadily to himself, "Yes, my lord, No, my lord. Yes, my lord. No, my lord."

"Who are you talking to?" Jim asked.

"The Bishop."

"But he isn't here."

"And a good thing too—," and he gave a violent kick to the generator which responded with a surprised wheeze and a chug-chug. Then he hurried to the vicarage, washed the grease from his hands and face, got into his surplice and went to the church where the congregation was waiting. "And God said, let there be light, and there was light."

In the last week of the month Mark neglected his boat and paid for it heavily. He and Jim had returned from the patrol and had just tied up at the float when the radio-telephone began to beep, and they were summoned back to one of the other villages, where three children, left alone in their cedar house for a few moments, had tipped over a kerosene lamp and been burned to death.

On the way back from the funeral on a rainless night, the wind blowing and the tide running, the engine died. Frantically Jim worked on the filter while Mark tried to keep the boat from the rocks, and when the filter was cleaned and the engine caught, he knew that curious change of tempo—one moment every breath a prayer and the next moment, the tension gone, and the two of them joking. The next day he knew also the exhaustion which is the price of courage.

When the weather turned cold, the trip upriver became torment. One afternoon a violent wind caught them in the open boat, the sleet blown vertically across the mountain sides. It cut their faces and blew an empty oil drum and the mail sack from the boat. When they reached the vicarage, they sat with their feet propped in the oven door of the old stove, sure that they would never know what it was to be warm again.

Mark wrote to the Bishop: "I have learned little of the Indians as yet. I know only what they are not. They are none of the things one has been led to believe. They are not simple, or emotional, they are not primitive." The Bishop wrote back: "Wait—you will come to know them."

But his acquaintance had widened now. He knew the young hand-logger who took his four children in a little open boat to the school at Echo Bay each morning and home again each afternoon, and sometimes he shared dinner with him and his fine brood at their float house on the edge of the chuck. He had visited the logging camps, and never did he pass the float house of Calamity Bill without looking to see if smoke was coming from his chimney and his ancient donkey engine was wheezing in the spruce. At sixty-five, Calamity climbed four thousand feet each day straight up the mountain side to cut his timber, and three times he had ridden his gear down into the chuck. When Mark stopped to ask how things were, the reply never varied, "Calamitous," and when Calamity Bill asked if he might come aboard, Mark's reply never varied either, "Yes, if you take off your cork boots."

One day in the church he remembered the organ, and he sat down and pumped the pedals and very tentatively, as if he didn't care at all, he pulled out a stop and poked a key and was rewarded by a fine, round tone. That night, one of the Indian women who had studied music at the school of Alert Bay, practised the hymns which were to be sung at Christmas, and an old brown bear, hibernating under the church, awoke, and the Indian hounds heard him and began to worry him. In the night the village suddenly exploded into sound, and Mark put on his slippers, threw a robe over his pajamas and dashed out to collide with a huge dark shape. He made two complete circles of the vicarage.

The next morning Chief Eddy stopped him on the path.

"I don't believe the Bishop would want you chasing bears around the vicarage in your pajamas."

"But I wasn't. You have it all wrong. The bear was chasing me."

Christmas was a busy time in the village. The churches in Vancouver sent toys which the women sorted into packs, not only for the village children, but for those at the logging camps, the isolated float houses on Mark's patrol. Ten days before Christmas Mark and Jim delivered the gifts, visiting the other villages, and each lonely float, in and out the inlets, travelling usually by compass, often with the bow awash, and always with the mountains thick with snow. Wherever there were children Jim wore the ancient Santa Claus suit and lifted the pack of toys on his back while the children waited on the float to welcome them, to arrange the boats so they could tie up. And after the carols were sung, and the gifts given, always Mark set up the portable altar for the simple service, and when they were pulling away, always he looked back to see some little girl clutching the rag doll to be cherished all year long.

They returned to the village Christmas Eve, with no time for dinner, and a hundred details to be checked before the midnight service. At eleven Mark was still trying to extract a little more heat from the fat round stove in the church. Hurrying back to the vicarage, he washed the soot from his hands, put on his vestments, and returned to the church to check the wine and the chalice, to toll the bell, to light the candles.

Then all was ready. He was alone, waiting in

the hushed silence with the candlelight shining on the golden eagle and on the sad eyes of Christ holding the little lamb, and it seemed to him the little church waited also.

He walked slowly down the center aisle, and not wanting to open the door until the very last minute for fear of losing the precious heat, he walked to the window at the left of the door and stepped without expectation into one of those moments that is suspended between time and space and lingers in the mind.

The snow lay thick on the shoulders of the Cedar-man; the limbs of the young spruce bent beneath its weight. He saw the lights of the houses go out, one by one, and the lanterns begin to flicker as the tribe came slowly, single file along the path to the church. How many times had they travelled thus through the mountain passes down from the Bering Sea?

He went to the door and opened it, and he stepped out into the soft white night, the snow whispering now under the footfalls. For the first time he knew them for what they were, the people of his hand and the sheep of his pasture, and he knew how deep was his commitment to them. When the first of the tribe reached the steps, he held out his hand to greet each by name. But first he spoke to himself, and he said, "Yes, my Lord."

PART TWO

The depth of sadness

EIGHT

Now for the first time since Mark's coming, the whole tribe was in residence and all the men were home from the fishing. Three days before Christmas, one of the seiners had brought the young people—those in their teens—from the church residential school at Alert Bay, and two of the largest canoes had met them at the float and brought them upriver. They had arrived at slack tide before the snowfall, the canoes grounding on the sandbars, the men climbing out into the icy water to shove, and push, to carry the girls to the bank, everyone laughing and the girls clutching the presents they had made at school for their parents. Mark had thought he had never seen such a joyous burst of bright-eyed youth.

But after Christmas, when the snow turned to slush and the rain fell, the children were kept inside and the men played La-hell in the social hall long into the night, Mark felt a strange little wind of dissent which seemed to whisper in the firs, to precede him, to follow him wherever he went.

He spoke of it to old Peter, the carver, who was down with a cold.

"Peter, what is it? What is this unease that is now in the village?" and the old man looked at him long and carefully before answering.

"It is always so when the young come back from the school. My people are proud of them, and resent them. They come from a far country. They speak English all the time, and forget the

words of Kwákwala. They are ashamed to dip
their food in the oil of the óolachon which we call
gleena. They say to their parents, 'Don't do it that
way. The white man does it this way.' They do not
remember the myths, and the meaning of the totems. They want to choose their own wives and
husbands."

He faltered as if what he was going to say was
too painful to utter.

"Here in the village my people are at home as
the fish in the sea, as the eagle in the sky. When
the young leave, the world takes them, and dam-
ages them. They no longer listen when the elders
speak. They go, and soon the village will go also."

"Kingcome will be one of the last to go, Peter."

"Yes, but in the end it will be deserted, the totems will fall, and the green will cover them. And
when I think of it, I am glad I will not be here to
see."

On the little organ in the church Mark had left
a carton of books his sister had sent for Christmas. One day he noticed the lid of the carton was
up and a book missing. The next day the book
was back and another gone, and when he went
into the church on the third day, one of the boys
who was home from school was sitting on the
bench by the organ reading.

It was Gordon, whose father had been lost in a
heavy sea in the Queen Charlotte Straits. He
looked up. He stood up and came forward with
the book. He was not embarrassed. He had even
forgotten to be shy.

"This word," he said eagerly, "what does it
mean?" and Mark explained the meaning and he
said, "I have some other new books you might en-
joy seeing. I'll leave them here for you."

He took over the books the next afternoon and

found the boy waiting. On the pew beside him was a mask.

"It's the giant mask," Gordon said. "The thong that ties it on is broken. Peter is going to mend it for me. They will need it in the dancing."

"May I see it?"

The boy held it up.

"Yes. See how thin it is. The modern ones are thick." He added, shyly, "It is my great-grand-mother's hair."

The mask was black with red lips and abalone eyes. When Mark took it into his hands, he felt almost as if he held a strong, proud, living face, so beautifully was it carved.

"My father was offered three thousand dollars for it," Gordon said, "but we do not want to sell it."

"No—only to a museum where the world can see it—only then."

Just before the end of the holiday, Mark heard in the village the first sound from the world outside. A jet plane broke the sound barrier. At first he thought it was a slide on Whoop-Szo, and he ran out of the vicarage. The sound caught in the inlets, tossed from one steep mountain side to another, echoing and reverberating, and receding slowly to echo and re-echo far, far away. It lasted several minutes, and he looked around to see a curious sight.

None of the older Indians had come out, only the young, the children, running excitedly up and down the path, the young people in a group by themselves. And Gordon.

Gordon stood motionless, head up.

Mark went over to him slowly.

"When I was a small boy I used to visit my grandmother in one of the little prairie towns in the mid-continent," he said. "And the sound I listened for was the long, shaky whistle of the freight train in the night. It was the eeriest sound I ever heard, and it seemed to call to me from the big world, and even then I knew I would answer it. I would go. Is this not the way you feel now?"

The depth of sadness in the boy's eyes deepened, as Peter's had deepened when he spoke of his village, and he said, "Yes." That was all.

On Sunday after church the young people returned to school. Many of the tribe went to the river's edge to see them off in the canoes. And the young people regretted going and wanted to go, and the elders wanted to keep them and were relieved when they went. The little dissent went with them, and the village was at peace.

But not for long. When the January storms tempered a little, Mark managed to reach the other villages for the first time in a month, and he stopped at the float store to pick up the mail sack for the village.

On the evening of the day he returned, Keetah knocked at the vicarage to tell him that Mrs. Hudson, her grandmother, was ill.

He found the old matriarch sitting very straight by her fire, her breath coming in short gasps, and he knew her well enough by now to guess that Mrs. Hudson was more upset than ill. He asked how she was. She was bad. It was her heart again. She was sure of it—she was determined she was not long for this world.

"And what is it that has upset you?" he asked her, and Mrs. Hudson shook her head, making a strange little aye-aye-aye sound that must have come down through the centuries in a chant of sorrow, and she told him sadly that her granddaughter, Keetah's sister, had written (and he himself had brought the letter in the mail sack) that she was going to marry a white man.

"But this happens often and frequently very successfully. There are even white women who have married Indians and been asked to sit on the councils."

Mrs. Hudson did not hear him.

"She will no longer be an Indian. Legally she will be white. She will have no right to come here, except as a visitor."

"But you can go and visit her."

"Yes. And when we go, she will say, 'Not today, Grandmother. Come tomorrow. My husband is home today'. And her husband will say, 'Do not ask your grandmother tomorrow. I do not want my aunt to see her.' "

"No," Keetah said. "No. My sister will not leave us. My sister is not like that. I know her. She will never, never be ashamed of us."

Mrs. Hudson lifted her fine old head.

"Of this I'm not afraid," she said simply. "What I fear is that we will be ashamed of her," and she was silent.

Mark sat beside her. When her breathing had eased and quieted, he told her of the Navaho, one of the great, proud tribes who lived in the southwest of the United States, so many hundreds of miles distant.

"One of the great chiefs of the Navaho said to his tribe, 'We can hear the white man talking, but we cannot reach him. Education is the ladder. Take it.' "

Mrs. Hudson said, "You do not understand. My grand-daughter goes to a world of which she knows nothing. It will destroy her and I cannot help her. To watch her go is to die a little."

And Keetah took the old hands in hers and said, "She will come to us. I know she will come, and she will not change. You will see."

NINE

This was the time of year when the deepest beliefs of the tribe were relived in the dances; no stranger asked, no photographs permitted. When Mark walked along the path past the long house, he could see masks in readiness, but he asked no questions and was told nothing.

In January the men of the tribe went to Gilford village to dig clams, and returned to Kingcome each week-end. Now the tide dominated all life. When the tide was out, clamming was on. When clamming was on, all else waited, even church.

One late afternoon when Mark and Jim were going to the most remote of the villages, they were passed by seiners headed for Gilford, and Mark was asked by radio-telephone if he would hold Evensong in the long house before a dance-potlatch to be given that evening by an elder in preparation for his own death.

When they reached Gilford village, many boats were tied up at the float, and when they entered the long house, more than three hundred Indians were waiting, the old carved house posts casting their shadows by lantern light, and by the light of the fire burning on the dirt floor in the center of the great room. And when Evensong was over and coffee was served, Mark saw that almost all of the tribe from Kingcome was here. With Keetah was her sister.

She was a pretty girl, her hair carefully cut and waved, her fingernails red, the heels of her slippers very high, and on her face that radiance of fulfillment, of all the wonders of the new life she was about to enter.

The two sat apart, talking earnestly, and though Mark could not hear the words, he was sure he knew them:

"Nothing will change. Tell me—tell me you don't feel I have deserted you."

"Of course not. You know that. I want you to go."

He watched their faces, and he knew each meant desperately what she said because they loved each other, and deep inside surely each knew the words were false, that the true words were those unspoken. Which was the braver, the one who left, or the one who stayed?

He said to Jim, "Which is the man Keetah's sister is going to marry? Is he here? I want to meet him."

"There is only one stranger. He is with the men from the forestry boat who are friends of the tribe." But in the flickering light of the fire and the lanterns Mark could not see clearly the face.

Then the potlatch began. In the back of the room was the orchestra—the hollow log with the painted ends which was the drum, propped on a wheel barrow, and the older men with the carved batons and the ancient rattles. The elder pounded on the ground with his long talking stick and welcomed the guests in Kwákwala and the orchestra began its rhythmic beat.

The women danced first, dressed alike in their red and black ceremonial blankets, with the two-headed serpent on the back or the fir tree outlined in handmade buttons. They turned right because the wolf turned right. When they shook their head-dresses, the air was filled with duck down, and the light caught on the blankets, the ermine-tailed robes and the spread aprons.

Then came the Grouse Dance, brought to the tribe by marriage from River's Inlet. When the elder introduced it, Jim translated his words:

"A little boy went to the woods to snare grouse and he was sure he had caught one because he could feel it pulling and jerking. But each time he lost it, and thought someone had taken it. The little boy lay down under a fir and went to sleep, and he could hear the grouse still drumming in the snare. This dance is his dream.

"Now watch carefully. The first character wears the door mask, and when it opens the grouse will enter calling softly. If you were an Indian walking beside a stream in the woods, knowing the woods as only an Indian knows them, everything you saw would come to life in this dance with all its meaning and its beauty."

The dance lasted three hours, and there were twenty-six characters, each with his masks, his songs and his dances. In came the old stump looking for its trunk, a little green spruce growing from its top. In came the mossy log, the fish swimming upstream, the long face, the laughing face, the giant and the skull of the man lost in the woods. Through it all the Indians sat without sound or movement, utterly attentive.

Last was the Moon Dance, performed in pantomime by two men, the Full Moon and the Half Moon. Which would come out tonight? "I will come out tonight. I am more powerful than you." "But I will stay out longer." They taunted each other, fingers to noses, and this time the audience shrieked with laughter, taunting each in turn, and applauding the favourite.

When the dance was over there were refreshments and gifts of china, linen and cutlery, and a fifty-cent piece for each guest except the family of the host.

"Where is the man Keetah's sister is to marry? I cannot find him," Mark asked Jim.

"He is gone. Keetah's sister is taking him to Kingcome tomorrow. You can meet him there."

They walked down the wet, dark path to the float, climbing over the railing and the deck of a seiner to reach their boat, and in the galley they discussed the potlatch. Was it true that in the old days the gifts had been so lavish they had beggared whole families and tribes, and made others rich?

Jim agreed it was true. "Even when I was a small boy stoves, refrigerators and washing machines were given as gifts. It is true that families gave all they had. But when the government forbade the great dance-potlatches, it gave us nothing to take their place, and changed the deepest purpose of our being. Once they were like the coronations of a king, or the inauguration of a president. They were the great rituals of my people, solemn and important. Now the meaning is gone."

"But Jim, isn't it true they were based on a chief's desire to shame his rival, even if it meant his tribe and his children went hungry?"

"Yes, and it was based also on generosity. My people have forgotten how to give. You do not understand how it was once. When I was seven my grandfather taught me my family's dances, and he gave a dance-potlatch in my honor, and asked the tribes of the other villages. Whether they came was not important. It would have been discourteous not to ask them.

"The guests were billeted in the houses of

Kingcome, twenty or thirty to each house, to be fed, to be cared for, and boats came up the inlet, and the canoes brought the guests up the river. Each night one of my relatives gave a great feast of seal, duck or salmon, and a tremendous quantity of gifts was brought from Alert Bay. Each night in the big house there was dancing."

"Did you dance the Grouse Dance?"

"No, I danced the hamatsa. I remember that for three days my mother kept me shut in my room because the young man bewitched by the cannibal spirit must not be seen until he returns from the woods. I did not understand this and I resented it. On the night of the dance my family hid me in the woods, and when it was dark, I returned to the village calling the hamatsa cry. I have never forgotten it. It was the greatest moment of my life."

At dawn with the tide, the forestry boat and the seiners of the guests from the other villages left Gilford. At eight, Mark was summoned by radio-telephone to Turnour Island to transport a sick child to the hospital at Alert Bay, and when this was done, a gale was blowing, and it was too rough to return to Kingcome, so they tied up at the dock, the boat rolling in the swell.

The next morning after breakfast they started home, the wind still strong, the sky leaden, the snow thick on the mountains. When they came up the inlet they knew that the tribe had returned for the week-end; the float was thickly moored with boats.

It was very cold on the river, as it was always bitterly cold on the river in the winter. Mark could feel the wind biting through his parka, and because the tide was wrong, they grounded and had to pull the boat over a sandbar. When at last they waded ashore in front of the vicarage, they knew at once something was wrong.

Farther down the river's bank they saw a group of the oldsters packing one of the larger canoes with great bundles of clothing as if for a long trek. Mrs. Hudson was one of them and when she saw them, she did not speak.

The village was very quiet, as it had been the day Mark had arrived. But its silence lacked peace. Although this was a Saturday and the children were out of school, not a child showed, no Indian hound came running to greet them.

Mark motioned to Jim that he was going on to the vicarage, and Jim nodded, and said, softly, "I will find out. I will come and tell you," but when he came to the vicarage, it was a long time before he spoke.

"Keetah's sister brought her man to the village the morning after the potlatch. He had his own boat, and her family was proud she had come, and welcomed him. While she showed the women her red fingernails and her new clothes, and told them of her new life, her man was with the men of the family."

"Yes. And what did he do, Jim?"

"He gave them liquor. When Gordon's uncle was very drunk, he sold the giant mask. The white man paid fifty dollars for it, and the uncle wrote him a bill of sale. In the morning before it was light, the white man left, and the girl with him."

"It is possible she did not know of it."

"Her family does not think so. The old of her family are leaving. They are leaving in shame and sadness. They are going to a deserted village."

"But how will they live?"

"As my people have always lived. They will live on fish, and clams, and seaweed. Later they will pick berries."

"I must stop them."

"You can't stop them."

"Then I must go to them. I must talk to them."

"It won't help."

When Mark walked along the bank to the place where the canoe waited, he knew it was useless. They were ready to go—the old of Keetah's family, warmly wrapped against the cold, and sitting very straight on the narrow wooden seats. As he approached, Keetah and Mrs. Hudson came slowly through the black sands, stopped, and Mrs. Hudson lifted her proud old face and spoke to him slowly.

"What have you done to us? What has the white man done to our young?" and they waded into the icy water and climbed into the canoe, and because, to keep them here, someone had removed the outboard motor, one of the old men poled into the center of the river where the current took them, the paddles lifting and falling. Not even Keetah looked back.

They were larger than themselves. They belonged to the great and small hegiras of the self-exiles of this earth, clinging fiercely to a way that is almost gone, as the last leaves fall at last gently and with great pride.

"What have you done to us?"

The words lingered in the wind, in the spruce, in the drizzle that had begun to fall, and Mark turned from them in pain and saw old Marta. He said, "Marta, what can I do?" and she said, "You can wait," and he stumbled past her and up the path and into the church.

That evening he wrote the Bishop and when

the answer came two weeks later, he took it to the church, afraid to open it. Had he failed? Was it his fault?

The letter was short: "I think it is time you knew of Tagoona, the Eskimo. Last year one of our white men said to him, 'We are glad you have been ordained as the first priest of your people. Now you can help us with their problem.' Tagoona asked, 'What is a problem?' and the white man said, 'Tagoona, if I held you by your heels from a third-story window, you would have a problem.' Tagoona considered this long and carefully. Then he said, 'I do not think so. If you saved me, all would be well. If you dropped me, nothing would matter. It is you who would have the problem.' "

TEN

In the cold, blustery days of February and March, when the men could not pursue the fish and the game, the life of the tribe turned in upon itself. The faces, once so much the same, grew clearly defined. Even Mark's ear had begun its attunement to the strange tongue. One week-day when the men were away clamming, and the younger matrons gathered at Marta's house to make new altar cloths, he dropped in to find them, heads bent to their work, talking softly in Kwákwala, and he realized, with almost a sense of shock, that the words no longer sounded like the click of knitting needles, and that they were speaking of him.

"Wait a minute," he said. "I didn't say that at all," and they looked up startled, then burst out laughing, and never, never again did they discuss him in Kwákwala in his presence.

When Ellie, the lost one, slipped home to her father's house before daylight, Mark knew now from whence she came, and when Ellie's mother sat sewing with the other women, totally unresponsive, in her vague, sweet way, Mark knew also that she was probably in a drunken stupor because Sam had beat her again.

Twice, when Mark did not need him on the boat, Jim left the village, and though he did not say so, Mark knew he had gone to see Keetah and the oldsters of her family.

"And how is Keetah?" he asked him.

"I told her that someday she would marry me, and that I would build her a fine house with a pink bathtub. No woman in the tribe has seen a pink bathtub."

"And what did she say?"

"She said I had no manners. She said when I want coffee, I bang on the table. She said I want a wife only to keep my house," and he laughed, then sobered.

"She is worried about her sister. All the time she is worried. It is more than two months and there is no word of her. There is no word at all."

"I am going to Alert Bay to see if there is any way I can get Ellie away from her parents and into the residential school. We will ask the RCMP there to find the sister."

In Alert Bay Mark visited the residential school and saw Gordon and the older children from the village who were there. At the headquarters of the RCMP Mark discussed the problem of Ellie with the sergeant in charge of the detachment, a man past middle age and wise, and from him Mark learned that to take Ellie from her parents without their consent was not easy. Then Mark told the sergeant about Keetah's sister, the older man listening carefully and without interruption.

"It is possible the man learned of the giant mask from some dealer who had tried to buy it," he said. "The dealers have a genius at knowing when the fishing is poor, which family is needy. With the Indians it is easy come, easy go. This goes back to the days of the great potlatches. They do not budget what they have, and even when times are excellent, they get into debt. It is then the dealers pick up their best carvings."

"I cannot believe the girl had any part of it. Her family is one of the finest in the village."

"Then there was trouble when she found out about it. I'll watch for her. I doubt if the man has married her. When he tires of her, she will be alone in a world for which she has no preparation. I'll find her."

In late March the tribe prepared for the coming of the óolachon, the candlefish, a season so deep in the tradition of the people that all the taboos and superstitions were remembered, and followed. No pregnant woman must cross the river. No body must be transported upon it. The chief of the tribe must catch the first fish.

On the night before the run began, there was a great feast in the social hall to which everyone came—except the school teacher, of course—and when the meal was done, the chief related the first myth of the óolachon:

"And Khawadelugha, the older brother, built his house here at Kingcome and carved its house posts with human figures, and one day when he walked to the river's edge he saw many small fish in the river and he was afraid. But the man who came from the moon said to him, 'Fear not. This fish will come year after year, and it will be the great wealth of your tribe,' and the fish was the óolachon, and the older brother called his tribe the Tsawataineuk, which means the people of the óolachon country."

T. P., the elder, related the second myth:

"And one year the óolachon did not come, and the young laughed, and cared not. One of the old men painted his canoe red, and he paddled toward Knight's Inlet until he came to Twin Falls where the óolachon were living. 'What do you want?' asked the óolachon. 'Come back to the river. Treat the young as they have treated me.' And the óolachon said, 'Have you brought eagle

feathers and goat fat?' 'Yes, I have them here.'
'Then return to your river and prepare your nets,'
and the old man did so, and the good members of
the tribe filled their nets with óolachon, but the
nets of the bad ones broke."

The next day the men placed their nets in the
river, gathering them in by canoe, and the
brailing began, shoulders lifting and falling, and
the air filled with the mewing of thousands of
gulls, and the little children leaning over the bank
to catch the fish in tins.

The males who came up the shallow side of the
river were dried on V-frames, smoked and canned.
But the females, richer in fat, who came up the
far, deep side of the river were rendered into
gleena in huge wooden vats over a small slow fire.
Day after day after day it lasted, and when Mark
escaped on the boat to another village, he found
the odour had permeated his clothes and went
with him, and when he returned and the render-
ing was over, it lingered.

One day the RCMP sergeant came unexpect-
edly up the river in a small boat, and Mark saw
him from the vicarage and went to the river's
edge to meet him.

"I've been dreading that smell all day," said the
RCMP officer cheerfully. "It's just as bad as I
remembered it. You know, when I was younger—and considerably more stupid—I came once
to take pictures of the óolachon fishing. I knew the
Indians did not permit pictures, but I figured they
couldn't stop me."

"And did they?"

"Oh, no, they were polite. They welcomed me.
They helped me back to my boat. But you know,
in doing so, one of the young men managed to

drop my camera in the river. All the way down the path to the float I was sure I could hear them laughing, and when I got home I found I had to bury my uniform and pay for a new one myself."

Mark led him to the vicarage, put on the coffee pot and prepared sandwiches, and when they had finished lunch at the kitchen table—the rain pattering on the roof—the sergeant took a photograph from his pocket.

"Is this the girl? Look at it carefully."

Mark did so.

"Yes. There's no doubt about it. This is Keetah's sister."

"The man didn't marry her. When she found out about the mask, she objected, I suppose. He left her in Vancouver, penniless, and he disappeared. I don't suppose she'd ever seen a paved street, or a train, or a telephone. There was no place for her to go, no work she was trained to do. She drifted to the only place where she was welcome."

"A beer parlour?"

"Yes. The money men paid her kept her alive. No one knew to what tribe she belonged. Even if she'd had the money to charter a plane, I suppose she would have been ashamed to return to her village. Soon she was taking dope—it's what is apt to happen—and one night she took too much, deliberately, probably, though we'll never know. You're sure of the identification?"

"Yes, I'm sure, but I'd like Jim to see the picture also. He's not here today."

"Dead in three months—well, it doesn't take long. You'll tell the family?"

"I'll have Jim tell them."

Mark went with the sergeant to the river's edge

and watched his boat head downstream to the inlet. He did not know that when he turned back in his own eyes was the depth of sadness which he had begun to understand.

ELEVEN

With spring the leaden skies broke, the winds lightened, the rains softened, and the eagles and the robins returned to the village. High in the skyways wild geese called exultantly on their first early passages back from the south, the wise old crow cawed over the river, his wings flapping loosely and slowly, and the sleek black raven, who stayed all year, nested in the tall alders.

With spring the first buds began to swell, and the fresh green needles of the spruce. The bracken and the fern reached out the tips of tender fronds, the devil's club put out small new leaves for the deer to nibble, and the bears emerged from their dens, thin, blinking in the light.

In May all the men readied the boats for the fishing, and the banks were piled with gill-nets to be mended, their white and green floats fresh with paint.

In May the boats left to gig for halibut, Mark and Jim accompanying them for two days' fishing in Knight's Inlet, a wild, lovely and lonely land, the boat rolling in the tidal sweep, the seals disputing each fish. When Mark and Jim returned to the village, they brought with them an orphaned baby seal, who repaid his bottle feedings by dusting the floors of the vicarage carefully with his flippers. When he was old enough, Mark taught him to swim in the river and let him go.

In June the men of the tribe went north to gillnet for salmon in River's Inlet. Now Mark was busier in the village than he had ever been, picking up the freight, the mail, the supplies; handling any accident or emergency that occurred in the village.

One night in early June he awakened to the sound of feet running on the path, to the calling of his name and fists pounding on the door.

"Come quickly—come quickly."

He pulled on his pants and his shoes in the dark, and snatched his jacket, and followed the Indian who had come to summon him into the night to the house of Gordon's mother, up the steps and in the door.

All the relatives waited in the front room, the dark eyes of the children big with wonder. Mark pushed past them and went into the bedroom.

On the blood-soaked bed lay Gordon's mother. At forty-six she had borne her sixth child, which Marta held wrapped in a blanket. All the other births had been normal, and although the native mid-wife was absent from the village, no difficulty had been expected. But this was a breech birth. This was abnormal and even Marta was afraid to have anything to do with the abnormal because of the RCMP.

"She is bleeding to death," Marta said, "and there is no time to get help."

Mark took the woman's cold hand. The nails were white, the face ashen, and the eyes fixed on his face. He bent to her.

"Help Gordon get an education," she whispered. "He will need it."

"I will."

He held her hand until she died, and she died quietly and quickly. Then Marta cleared the front room of the relatives, and gathered the woman's children to the bedside where Mark said the Lord's Prayer.

Then they closed the bedroom door, because nothing could be done until the RCMP came, and they undressed the children and put them to bed. In the early dawn Mark and Jim went down the river to the boat to summon the police by radio-telephone and to send word of the death to the fishing boats in River's Inlet, so that the male relatives would come, stopping first at Alert Bay for the box in which to bury her.

When Mark returned to the village he noticed there were no professional wailers with scratched faces and he asked Marta why.

"She did not want them."

The RCMP came in the late afternoon by boat. He was the constable who had come for the weesa-bedó, as cold as the first time. Mark showed him the body and called the relatives that he might take the statement of each. When the questions were all asked and the statements signed, the constable issued the burial permit and left.

Then he and Marta were alone in the bedroom with the ugliness of death.

"Marta, what do we do now?" and she told him.

Mark closed the eyes, straightened the limbs and packed the orifices of the body against further seepage. He and the men of the family carried the body into the tiny vestry of the church, and Marta and the women bathed it, powdered it, and dressed it in its best clothes, and when the box came from Alert Bay, they put the body in it, closed it, and they placed it by the golden eagle, by the Christ with the dark, sad eyes holding the little lamb.

Everyone in the village shared the death. Here death could not be hidden or pushed aside. Here death was normal. The women were busy in their kitchens preparing food for the relatives and the guests who would come from the other villages. Two canoes, spliced together, bore the coffin carefully up the river. The older men went to the new burial ground, a mile from the village, to dig the grave, and the older boys followed them, cutting away the bracken, the devil's club, that had grown over the narrow path. Even the small children went into the woods to seek wild flowers and green fern fronds which the younger women needed for the wreaths. The older women swept and dusted the church. And Jim and Peter, the carver, made the long trip to the residential school to bring Gordon.

On the morning of the funeral Mark tolled the bell, and the tribe gathered in the church for the service. When it was over, he left the church first, leading the way down the aisle, down the steps, to the path that led through the deep woods to the new burial ground. Behind him six men carried the burial box, another six following to take their places when they tired. Behind them, single file, came the tribe.

Sometimes the path was so narrow that the men who carried the box had to tilt it, maneuvering it carefully through the trees, and in the deep shadowy woods there were puddles that never dried, and here Mark held up his cassock and felt on his bare head the wet drops that fell from the dark firs from the last rain.

An eagle accompanied them, soaring and returning in great, wide arcs, and once they surprised a doe and her little fawn. The doe carefully nudged the fawn off the path, keeping herself between it and them. When the path made a turn, Mark looked back and saw the tribe stretched through the cedar and the hemlock, coming slowly and silently, except for the footfalls on the soft duff.

Thus he went, the air fresh from rain and filled with the sweet smell of fir, the sky blue and white with cloud. On the top of Whoop-Szo above the timber line, snow lay waiting for the warm suns of July to send it sliding downward with a rumble that would fill the village. And it seemed to Mark that death belonged here as the mountains belonged, as the eagle belonged, and the little scurrying squirrels that peered at him from the fir boughs. And it seemed to him that the ugliness of death was as unimportant here as the fir needles which made the path soft beneath his feet, or last year's windfall in the thick underbrush.

When Mark led the way into the glade of the new burial ground, the six men set down the box, the tribe gathering quietly in a circle around it. The committal was brief, and when Mark had said the last words, "Rest eternal grant unto her, O Lord, and let light perpetual shine upon her," each man of the tribe helped fill the grave with a spade of earth while the women sang in Kwákwala the first hymns the tribe had been taught sixty-five years before.

Then the wreaths were placed on the grave. T. P., the elder, stepped forward. He spoke in the ancient Elizabethan Kwákwala and the children, tugging at their parents, asked, "What does he say?" and though Mark did not ask him, Jim translated.

"He says she was a mother of the tribe. She spoke little and only when asked, and the men listened to her counsel. . . . He says she was one of the first to choose her own husband . . . and he says that her husband, as a boy, was the first to have shoes, and that he hung them on a tree for all to see but did not wear them. . . . And he says she was good."

Mark walked back to the village with Gordon and when the path widened enough that they could walk side by side, they talked briefly.

"Now I will have to come home and care for my brothers and sisters, and for the new one."

"No—I have given this much thought. The older ones will go to the residential school where you can be with them. The younger children we will care for here, and the new one also. Your mother wanted you to get an education. I told her I would help you."

The next morning Mark stepped from the vicarage into the first lovely day of summer. Sitting on a log near the river's edge was Marta, the small boy and girl who had been his first friends kneeling at her feet. As he approached he could hear her singing to them in Kwákwala.

Wake up, small daughter, wake up.
The sun is high and the tide is out.
All the other children are playing in the water.
You will be the last.

The small boy cried in English, "My turn—my turn," and Marta sang the next song for him.

I want to pursue the swimmer like my father.
I want to hunt the bear like my father.
When I am grown my father will lack nothing.

Then Marta saw Mark standing there, the weariness plain on his face. She shooed the children away with a gesture, and Mark sat down on the log beside her.

"You are tired," she said.

"Yes."

They sat then without talking, listening to the mewing of the gulls, watching two sleek black ravens in the alders across the river. Presently Mark saw a sight he could not at first believe—he saw Mrs. Hudson come to the beach, wade into the water, climb into a canoe, and pole into the middle of the river to dump her garbage.

"The old have returned," he said cautiously, "I did not see them at the funeral."

"You did not see them because there were so many."

"They are leaving again?"

"No, they have returned to stay."

He was so grateful he did not trust himself to speak. Then Chief Eddy came along the beach by the river's edge, and saw them sitting there on the log and drew close.

"Mark," he said, "the men have asked me to tell you that when you are ready to build a new vicarage, they will help you. It would be wise to get it up before the rains come."

"I will write the Bishop today. Will you tell the men I am grateful?"

Then they were alone. But there was a difference now. The cautious waiting was over. That night Mark wrote to the Bishop and the Bishop's answer affirmed it. "You suffered with them, and now you are theirs, and nothing will ever be the same again."

PART THREE

Che-kwa-la

TWELVE

The men of the village tore down the vicarage. The old boards were cut and shared with all for firewood. The foundation for the new house was prepared according to the blueprints which the Bishop sent, and Mark went to live at Marta's house where she spoiled him with Indian delicacies, berry sprouts cooked with alder and salal, and salmon eggs baked with milkweed, topped with fern. Usually Jim dined with them, and often Keetah, and the times Mark liked the best were the long summer twilights when the elders dropped in to speak of the old culture.

They were all alike, the old, tied by a common bond. "We are the only ones left who remember the old ways and if we do not speak now, they will be forgotten."

Sometimes Mark was appalled at how much was gone, how little they remembered from their long past, and he encouraged Keetah to write down the small treasures that floated up in the old minds:

"And the little girl of the family took the bones of the first halibut to the water's edge, and gave them back to the sea, and she said, 'Come again, Mr. Halibu-u-u-u-t, come again next year.' "

"And the young men strolled through the village singing the old love songs, and the songs were always of absence and of sorrow, and they spoke from the heart."

"I went with my mother to strip the bark from

the young cedar and I remember that she spoke to the tree. She said, 'Forgive me because I seek your dress. I will not leave you naked', and she told the tree what she would make from the bark—a blanket, and a pillow for her baby's head."

"I was afraid of the hamatsa dance. I was afraid of the men who looked so fierce with their heads wreathed with hemlock, and their bearskins tied with cedar rope."

"We went in the sixty-foot canoe to buy gifts for my uncle's potlatch, and we spent all we had, and gave away all our blankets. That winter we were cold and the children cried."

The first week-end Gordon was home from fishing with his uncle, he came to Marta's house, bringing three boys who had been with him at the Indian school and who wished also to board with a white family and go to school in a white man's town.

When Gordon was there, Jim did not come or the elders. Gordon was not interested in the past. His mind reached only ahead with that urgent intensity which makes youth seem selfish, and is so necessary to difficult accomplishment.

"Do you think I can do it?" he would ask Keetah. "What do you think?" and she would answer, "I know you can. Of course you can."

When Gordon returned to the fishing, the elders returned, Keetah's dark head bent again to her notebook, and Jim reasserting the old role of the tribal male, pounding on the table when he wished coffee, and Keetah, putting down her pen to wait on him without a look, without a word.

When the freight boat deposited the new prefabricated vicarage on the float at the end of the inlet, those men of the tribe who were not off fishing went by canoe to see and consult. There waited the vicarage—every beam, every shingle, every nail, to be carried up the wilful river. Even Calamity Bill came in his ancient row boat with its ancient outboard motor, and the younger hand-logger, the summer sun shining on his hard hat, and all of them nodded their heads and agreed that the easiest and the quickest way to get the makings of the vicarage to the village was to hire a forestry barge at a prodigious thirty dollars a day.

It took two days and two nights to transfer the lumber to the barge, to maneuver it carefully up the river, past the snags and the sandbars, and to unload it. Sometimes, at night, Mark would stop working a moment to watch. The whole tribe helped. Even some of the women waded into the cold water to help carry the larger pieces, while the small boys bent their backs to the kegs, and in the flickering lantern light Keetah's dark head bent to the coffee pot as she filled cups, and carried them to the river's edge. On the third morning the forestry barge was returned and the new vicarage lay on the green grass of the meadow.

"Now," said Chief Eddy, proudly, "we will put up the house."

For six weeks the village was filled with a constant activity. Every available man—and even some of the women—helped put up the new vicarage. It must be done before the heavy rains of August, and for another reason of which no one spoke. In August, for the first time, the Indian was to be permitted to buy liquor.

All day long and into the long twilight the sound of hammering continued, accompanied by laughter and the shouts of the men, and by the shuffling of feet under the loads of timber.

One July night the inlet became a small and

lovely city of lights. The gill-netters—a hundred and fifty of them—were fishing for salmon, drifting slowly with the will of wind and tide, their nets extended to the full twelve hundred feet, and the three lights on each ship rising and falling with the tidal sweep. And the villagers went by canoe to watch and marvel.

Now when Mark and Jim moved up and down the inlet in the little speed boat on patrol, they had to take care lest they foul the lines. Often men on the gill-netters yelled loudly and boisterously, "Watch where you're going, you fools. Look out for that net—," the finest words Mark had heard here because they could be said only by one friend to another which meant he was one of them.

When the gill-netting in the inlet was over, the little city of lights went out in the summer night, and the smaller children asked anxiously, "Where has it gone? Will it come again?" and the inlet was empty as the room is empty when the Yule tree is stripped and carried out into the rain.

These were the lovely days of summer; the water of the inlet deep green from the shadows of the spruce, the children in and out of the river all day long, agile as seals, and the village full of laughter.

When the new vicarage was done at last there was a brief respite until the new furniture, chosen by the wife of the Archdeacon at the Bishop's request, was delivered to the float to be carried up-river.

Mark and Jim took Marta, and the two children who had been his first friends, on a picnic. In a cove where there was a small sandy beach they spread their supper on a driftwood log, and in the long twilight, because it was a time of much phosphorescence, they lingered to watch the fish jump and fall back into pools of golden light. And the barefoot children ran backwards to watch their small footprints glowing in the dark sand.

When they returned up the river in the soft quiet night and reached the village, Mark carried the little girl ashore and Jim the boy, and when they delivered them to their parents, Mark walked alone by the river's edge, clinging to the lovely day. "Don't go—not yet—not yet—" but the day slipped away as fast as any other.

The freight boat dumped the new furniture on the float. The men brought it up the river and set it in place. The women pressed the new curtains and hung them, and the little children crept inside the new doors to touch nothing, to stand big-eyed and marvel, and the Bishop was asked to come bless the vicarage, a tribal feast planned in his honour.

The younger wives went at once to the house of Mrs. Hudson, sitting before her in a respectful circle, and they said in Kwákwala, "What shall we serve?"

"Barbecued salmon."

"How many?" and Mrs. Hudson considered it carefully and said, "Twenty."

"What vegetable?"

"Mashed turnips."

"How many?"

"Forty pounds."

The Bishop sent word that he would arrive on the hospital ship early on Sunday morning, and that he had asked six city rectors to join him in a retreat in the village, and that they would be deposited at Gilford Island by seaplane Saturday noon.

Mark and Jim met the clergy at Gilford village.

On the way to Kingcome, near Whale Pass, they saw a huge black bear swimming across the narrow channel, and stopped the boat and drew alongside. On an impulse, Jim picked up a line from the deck and tossed the noose neatly over the bear's head. Up came two huge claws and a furiously shaking black head, full of teeth, and emitting loud growls, and the town rectors began to laugh and yell, while Mark grabbed the axe, cut the rope, and the bear headed shoreward.

When they reached the home float and transferred to the canoes a heavy mist hung over the river. The landlubber clergy tried desperately to find a comfortable way to perch on the one-by-four crosspieces that formed the seats, the water gurgling ominously, Jim's torch seeking the log jams and the snags. When they reached the vicarage, Keetah and old Marta were waiting at the door of the new vicarage to ask, "And how did you like coming up our river?"

Two of the clergy stayed with Mark in the new vicarage, sleeping on the sofa, the big bed in the spare bedroom reserved, of course, for the Bishop, and the remaining four of the visitors were lodged in the homes of the Indians. In mid-morning of the next day, the hospital ship tied up at the float, and when the canoe came upriver with the Bishop, Caleb was with him, wading ashore in his ancient hip boots. But the Bishop had no Kingcome slippers and was carried piggyback to the bank.

For the service the church was filled. Caleb baptised two babies. The Bishop confirmed three of the younger Indians, and gave the sermon and blessed the vicarage. When it was done, he said to Marta, "Where was Mrs. Hudson?" and when Marta replied that Mrs. Hudson was ill, he said,

"Then I must take her communion."

The Bishop went first up the path through the woods carrying his staff, Mark following with the chalice and the paten. They found Mrs. Hudson propped on pillows, her breath coming in small, short gasps, and Mark, who had cherished the unchristian idea that Mrs. Hudson's old nose was badly out of place because the Bishop was housed in the new vicarage instead of her house, as had long been his custom, was ashamed of himself and sure she was about to die.

When they left, the Bishop stood a moment outside the door and he said loudly, "What a pity Mrs. Hudson will not be able to dance tomorrow after the tribal dinner. No one dances as well as Mrs. Hudson. No one."

That night the combined clergy prepared dinner in the new vicarage kitchen, and Mark told Caleb about the four boys who were going out to school.

"Have you found homes for them?" Caleb asked. "If not, I will help you. You don't want them with families who will say, 'Are they dirty? Do they steal?' I'll make the arrangements and you bring them to me."

In the morning the kitchen was turned into a clinic, busy with the doctor treating all assorted aches and pains. At noon one of the Indians broke his arm when the kicker on his canoe acted up, and he had to be taken to the hospital ship to have it X-rayed and set. In the afternoon the village was filled with the fragrance of the salmon barbecuing on the alder fires. The community feast was held in the social hall, and when it was over the visitors and the tribe moved to the ceremonial house. When the women began the dancing, there was Mrs. Hudson, turning right because the wolf turns right, the sequins of her ceremonial blanket shining in the firelight, her face pink with pleasure. And the Bishop leaned to Mark and said gently, "I have seen it happen many times. I cannot explain it."

Caleb and the clergy left the hospital ship at six the next morning, the sky leaden, the breeze cool. When the Bishop left at nine, an hour more suitable to his station, the rain was heavy. As he and Mark climbed into the speed boat, another passenger appeared. Dolores, one of the young Indian women, whose first baby was not due for a month, had started labour and asked to be taken to the hospital at Alert Bay.

They went downriver in a torrential rain, the young wife and the Bishop cowering under a polyethelene sheet. When they reached the boat at the float, they had to wait only moments before the tiny seaplane came, as ordered, to carry the Bishop to Vancouver Island.

The young bush pilot was properly appalled by the imminent prospect of birth.

"What'll I do?" he said to Mark. Mark said, "Nonsense. Just loop the loop—it'll all come out. Get going now." And he said softly to Dolores, "Hang on to it. Do you hear me?"

"Oh, I will, I will—."

"You are worrying because day after tomorrow the tribe will be able to buy liquor?" the Bishop asked Mark as he climbed on the plane.

"A little, my lord; I am afraid some of my best parishioners will end up in the gutter."

"The church belongs in the gutter. It is where it does some of its best work."

Then the little seaplane skittered across the water like a bug, lifted and turned. Mark saw Dolores' small determined smile. The young pilot

waved. The Bishop lifted his hand, as if in blessing. He was alone on the float there in the wilder-
ness, a drop of something wet on his cheek that
was not rain.

THIRTEEN

August began with floods. For days the rain poured down and the river rose until it lapped at the top step of the new vicarage, covering the path and the meadow, the villagers paddling from house to house by canoe. When the river went down, a small slide damaged the dam, and while the women carried water in pots and pails, Mark and the older men repaired the dam. In the night Mark could hear the footfalls of the men checking the moorings of the canoes, and he could hear the drip-drip of the rain, which had become a part of life itself, so that when it ceased, the world was filled suddenly with a strange, unnatural silence. Then the skies cleared, the sun shone, the weather turned suddenly warm, and the mosquitoes and the "no-seeums" emerged in hungry swarms.

August was a month of worry and waiting. Every time Mark went on patrol to the other villages, he returned filled with anxiety. At Gilford the captain of the freight boat told him the fishermen of the tribe had spent at least two thousand dollars on liquor in one week at Alert Bay. They had met other tribes with whom they had never been friendly, and there had been fights, even fights with knives, and it was said several Indians had gambled away their boats.

Coming home from Gilford one warm afternoon, Mark found a splendid, large American yacht tied at the float in the inlet. There was no one aboard, and when he and Jim moored their own boat and climbed into the speed boat, they could see through the portholes the rich polished helm, the gleaming mahogany of the main cabin with its elaborate bar.

When they came up the river to the village, a shabby speed boat was pulled up on the beach and a young logger in a plaid shirt perched on the bank, who explained that the yacht owner had paid him to bring his party here.

There were three women and four men, and as he walked up the path to the vicarage, Mark could hear chatter and gay laughter, and when he passed the vicarage, he could see them—the women in their tailored slacks and cashmere sweaters, the yacht owner in his white jacket and gold braided cap.

They were swatting mosquitoes and horse flies, gawking in the windows of the church, and the voices of the women had a shrill quality he had almost forgotten.

"Look—look at the funny man at the bottom of the totem."

When he approached and introduced himself, they were most affable.

"What are you doing here?" asked the yacht owner, and Mark said he belonged here; he lived here. And one of the women said, "How do you tell the Indians apart?" and Mark said, the same way she told her friends apart, because she knew them.

He showed them the village and he answered their questions, and, when they were ready to go, he went with them to the river bank. When the yacht owner saw his speed boat, he said, "I wonder if you would take us to the yacht in your boat? The mosquitoes are eating us alive, and the logger's tub is too slow. It would mean a little money in your collection plate." And Mark said, no, they would have to return the way they had come, and he noticed that Jim had picked up a stick and was drawing on the sands the picture of a dollar bill.

"If you come to southern California, you must look us up," said the wife of the yacht owner. "We will show you our big parish," and he knew he would never see it, and that she knew it also.

They climbed into the logger's boat and pushed off, and the river took them. They were on their way back to a life he no longer knew, as distant as another planet, and he was glad to see them go—and a little ashamed of it.

He looked at the picture in the sand.

"What does it mean?" he asked, and Jim answered, "It means an American stood here."

That week-end for the first time there was much drunkenness in the village. Three of the fishermen came home, reeling up the dark path. From Sam's house in the night came sounds Mark had never heard here, a woman's voice in a high, drunken giggle, and in the moonlight he saw Mrs. Hudson march down the path like a thunderhead and up the steps. Instantly the laughter stopped.

In the latter third of the month, an English woman anthropologist came to visit the village, housed, by arrangements of the Indian Agent with a couple who were among the very few of the tribe who were not Christians and did not attend church. When Mark went to call on her and offer any help he could, he was at once rebuked.

She was a large, mannish, gray-haired woman who informed him that her visit here was a fulfillment of a wish of many years standing.

"Since I was a girl," she announced, "I have

been interested in the culture of the Quacka-doodles."

Mark said hastily, "I had trouble with that word too. It took me a month to learn it. The Indians pronounce it Kwacutals."

"Young man, for the past century in England this band has been known as the Quackadoodles and as the Quackadoodles, it will be known for-ever."

"I beg your pardon."

Mark asked if she would like to see the church, and when they entered, she saw at once the new insulated sidings which had caused him so many blisters.

"How much better it would have been to have left the rude studding," she said sadly, and he told her that even with the plywood the flowers on the altar at Christmas had frozen solid in the water that held them.

She did not hear him. What a shame that Christianity had come here! If the white man had not intruded where he was not wanted, where he did not belong, even now, protected by the moun-tains and the river, the village would have re-mained a last stronghold of a culture which was almost gone.

Mark tried to say that no village, no culture, can remain static.

"I have often thought that if this lovely and magnificent land belongs to anyone, it is to the birds and the fish. They were here long before the first Indian, and when the last man is gone from the earth, it will be theirs again."

After this encounter Mark left the lady anthro-pologist alone. But he could see her sometimes, going around the village in her brogues and tweeds, with her notebooks and her pencils, asking innumerable questions of everyone. At the end of ten days, she knocked at the vicarage.

"I have completed my work except for one thing. The raven."

"What about the raven?" Mark asked.

"That's just it. There is a mystery about the raven they will not tell me. If I ask one of the Indians, he says he knows but he can't translate it. When I ask the chief, he says he knows, but the older Indians know better and I must ask them. And when I ask the older Indians, they say they knew it once and cannot remember."

Mark promised to help her, and went straight to Mrs. Hudson with his problem, who said she would arrange it.

"It is a long myth," said Mrs. Hudson, "and T. P. Wallace knows it well. He is going on a five-hour trip tomorrow on his son's seiner, and if the lady anthropologist cares to go along, the time should be ample."

The Englishwoman never mentioned the trip, and Mark did not question her, but late on the night of the day it was made, old T. P. came to the vicarage to apologize.

"We had bad luck. We went into Knight's Inlet and on the way back we hit a very strong tidal sweep."

"You told her the myth?"

"Certainly. I started the minute we left the float and I didn't reach the end until we returned. But you know, boss, she was so seasick, she didn't hear me. All she could say was, 'Oh, ghastly, ghastly.'"

On the afternoon the lady anthropologist left, the tide was out and the seaplane could not put down on the river, so Mark and Jim took her to the float in one of the canoes.

"The water's lower than it has been for some time," he explained. "Now, if we get stuck on a sandbar, you stay in the canoe. We'll get out and push."

The anthropologist said she would do her part. She wanted no favours.

"No, no—the water's very cold."

And, sure enough, the boat grounded and Mark climbed out in his rubber boots and Jim, also.

"Now?" asked the anthropologist, rolling up her slacks, and out she stepped—into a hole and up to her armpits.

When the seaplane arrived and took her, she did not wave, and they watched the plane disappearing into the blue sky.

"Oh, ghastly," Jim said with an exaggerated English accent. "Ghastly—ghastly."

But the vicar had a new word also.

"Quackadoodle, let's go home."

At the end of August Mark received a letter from the Bishop who wrote that he had been informed by the RCMP that the tribe had spent now a total of $6,000.00 on liquor at Alert Bay.

"When you bring the first four boys out to school, plan on at least three weeks' vacation. This will give the fishermen a chance to make their own peace with the old people. And when you return and the first man knocks at the vicarage to say he has no money to feed his family or to repair the outboard motor of his canoe, you will say, 'You will fish and hunt to feed your family. You were born with a paddle and a fish hook in your hand. Use them.'"

FOURTEEN

In the late summer Mark and Jim took the boat for its annual overhauling on the long journey to Vancouver. With them went the four boys who were to be the first of the tribe to attend the white man's school in a world of which they knew nothing and which knew nothing of them.

Chief Eddy took them in the largest canoe with all their assorted bundles and boxes, and the tribe gathered on the black sands by the river's edge to see them off.

"You will write. You will come home at Christmas," Keetah said to Gordon, and he answered, "I promise you. I will write. I will come on the seaplane," and his eyes were bright with eagerness, like the eyes of the three younger boys, and none knew that when the canoe left the shallows and the current took it, he was leaving his boyhood behind and would not find it again.

But the old knew it. The old knew this was another bit of the slow dying of all they held dear in their own race. And because he could not bear to see the look in the old eyes, Mark hurried the boys into the canoe, easing the tension with small jokes. Jim started the outboard motor, and they were off.

One afternoon on the trip down-coast they hid out a gale in a deserted village, the boys pitching horseshoes in a clearing white with broken clam shells. At night the boys slept on the floor, and at meals in the galley Mark drilled them in the little

amenities of the big wide world: "May I have another glass of milk, please?—Would you pass the
bread, please?—Excuse me.—I beg your
pardon.—How do you do?—And when you shake
hands, press a little." And he remembered that
none of them had ever seen a shower, and drew a
picture of one, explaining it carefully. "This is the
hot water faucet, and when you turn it on, be
careful not to scald yourself," and Gordon asked,
"But how do you wash your hands and face in this
little box without getting your clothes wet?"

When they had finished the small amenities, it
was Jim who introduced them to the larger ones.

"When somebody calls you a dirty Siwash,
what will you do?" When one of the younger boys
answered him, Mark said quickly, "No, you won't.
None of that. You will make a joke of it. You'll
laugh and you'll say, 'What's the matter, pale-
face?', and remember something: that in the
sports at school you'll be as good as any white boy
and far better than most, and they will respect it."

The trip down was full of laughter and anticipation, and when at last they entered the lovely
harbour of Vancouver, there stretched before
them was the first large city.

They slept on the boat, and by day, while the
work was being done on the engine, Jim and
Mark introduced them to the parks, the pave-
ments strangely hard to their feet, the noise new
to their ears.

Once Mark took them out to dinner to their first
large restaurant, and Gordon said to him, "They
are staring at us," and Mark answered, "Nonsense, they are staring at me and my clerical col-
lar." On the way back to the boat they passed
three young Indians, loud spoken, ill-kempt and
slovenly, and he felt the boys stiffen with enmity.

"What's the matter?"

"They belong to a southern tribe. We do not know them. We have never had anything to do with them."

Mark took his examinations to handle the boat alone. His sister, who was his only close relative, came from Victoria to meet him and they had a fine luncheon in one of the finest hotels. Mark's talk was almost entirely of the village, of the Indians, of the little amusing happenings. Since he was used to it, he did not heed, consciously at least, the sadness she could not keep back from her eyes.

When he looked up some of the friends with whom he had attended college, he realized with a shock that he no longer talked the same language. They spoke freely of their problems and assumed they were his also. Had he noticed how many young people there were now who seemed to find in life no challenge? And how did he handle the growing materialism in which so many people feel no need of faith and consider the church almost an anachronism? And Mark answered that in an Indian village the challenge was obvious to all, to stay alive men had to depend on each other, and that everyone came to church, even the agnostics and the atheists. They came out of respect for the church itself and for the man who served it, and because there were few settlers in a six thousand square mile area who had not been done kindness by the church, its hospital ship, its men, and repaid it.

On the last evening Mark had dinner with a professor under whom he had studied, the older man asking him many questions of his life in the village.

"You're growing more and more like Caleb," he

told Mark. "You've dropped yourself overboard in some quiet inlet, too busy living your faith to think of yourself at all. We'll have to watch you, Mark. You'll be wearing a white stole at Yuletide."

"With mud on my cassock? That's one place where you failed me. There was nothing in my training that told me how to remove mud from cassocks."

"I'll put it in the curriculum. Caleb spoke to the students last winter. The week before he came, we'd had a famous theologian whose words sent the students scurrying to their rooms to hassle half the night. But Caleb was like a cool wind from the north, or the smell of fir in the sun. No great theological problems. No debatable tenets. He spoke simply of his life on the up-coast, and often humorously. I remember watching the faces of the students as they listened, and I was sure I knew the look on the faces of the first ones who met long ago in some little hidden room in Antioch."

When the holiday was over, they started up-coast to Powell River. Now the boys had seen enough of the world to sense the size of the battle ahead, and they were like Jim the first night Mark had met him—quiet, poised, and proud. Even at dinner in the galley there was no joking, and when on the second day they tied up at the float at the marina, old Caleb was waiting.

"I hate good-byes," Caleb said to Mark. "Let's make this fast," and Mark agreed.

"I've found fine homes for you," Caleb told the boys. "A doctor and his wife are going to take Gordon. They have a son of their own and the doctor has a small cruiser he uses for week-ends. He can use a good hand. And as for you three—a widow's going to make room for you so you'll all be together. She has a big, old house and two grown children of her own. This morning she called to ask me what she could prepare for dinner that you would especially like. Nothing like a familiar dish to make a man feel at home. And when I said you'd like seaweed and óolachon, she laughed, and said she didn't have an óolachon in the house but did I think you'd settle for apple pie?"

When the boys had all their belongings moved to the float, there was one bad moment. Mark held out his hand to Gordon and he said, "You will be lonely, and you will be afraid sometimes. I was lonely, and I was afraid when I went to your village. Both are an inescapable part of every life." He shook hands with each of the boys very formally. He watched them pick up their luggage and follow Caleb up the ramp, like a small, proud army. Then he was in the cabin, starting the engine, while Jim coiled the lines. They were off. Neither looked back.

On the second day when they drew near the area of his patrol, Mark felt the quickening, the growing eagerness of one who comes home after an absence that seemed very long. How well he had come to know the landmarks; the turn at Broken Island. The last of the lights at Chatham Sound. The rock that was always covered with cormorants where he never failed to blow the whistle to watch them lift as one—and settle. He knew the pass where the porpoise was, and if he were blindfolded, surely he would know the place in the Johnstone Straits where the sea begins to roughen when the wind is against the tide. He knew the rocks that were marked on no chart as the Indian knew them, because he had scraped his keel on them on some dark night.

When they came into Kingcome Inlet and approached the float, he was like the man who comes to the door of his house, feels the weight of the day lift from his shoulders, and thinks, "Thank God, I'm home."

Then they were in the small boat going up the inlet into the river, past the log jams and the snags, toward the white-barked alders across from the village.

How had the drinking gone? In the entire holiday the question had been lying in his mind waiting an answer. But the village seemed utterly at peace. No one reeled down the path. No one lay inert, sleeping it off in the bushes. And Chief Eddy, who was painting his canoe on the bank, waved and came forward.

"How is it, Ed?"

"Okay, boss. Everybody's broke, but no one's dead. You might say it's steeled down, and it's all due to Sam."

To Sam, who had never done anything right in his life? Mark could not believe it.

"He collided with some fish. He made a lot of money. He spent most of it on liquor, and with what he had left he bought a washing machine, and brought it up the river in his canoe. But he was so drunk he hit the snags, tipped over, and lost it."

"I'm sorry to hear that."

"Did wonders for his wife, boss. You'd never know her. She beat him over the head with a skillet and locked him out of the house, and she wouldn't let him in until he agreed to let Ellie go out to school. I expect they'll be over to see you tonight."

"I'll be here, Ed."

When Mark entered the vicarage he saw that it

had been freshly cleaned and dusted. On the kitchen table was a loaf of bread, still warm from the oven. The Indians had known somehow he would return this day.

FIFTEEN

On the second night of Mark's return from his holiday, Marta asked him to dinner, and she did not ask Jim also, which was unusual.

"After the dinner the old will come," she told him. "They have something to request."

"You don't suppose they are still grieving about the drinking, or the boys going out to school," Mark asked Jim. "You don't suppose they are going to leave the village again?"

Jim did not think so.

"If this were it, I am sure I would be told. It is something which concerns only the old."

At dinner Marta did not mention what it was the elders wished. She asked of the holiday in Vancouver and she asked of Gordon and the boys.

"The younger ones will adjust more easily," Mark told her. "For Gordon it will be harder. He is much older than the boys he will meet at school. But he will endure, Marta, and he will win his battle."

After dinner there was a knock at the door and the elders entered: Mrs. Hudson, T. P., Peter the carver, and several others whom Mark did not know well, who still thought in Kwákwala, dreamed in Kwákwala, and spoke little English.

When they were seated there was a long silence, as the old watched Mark intently and soberly. It was not the drinking that had brought them here. It was not even the loss of the young. It was something that led back into the deepest beliefs of the tribe, and Mark sensed it and waited.

T. P. spoke for them.

"We have come about the ancient burial ground," he said. "Except for the weesa-bedó, it has not been used for many years."

"And you want the body of the weesa-bedó moved to the new graveyard. Is that it, T. P.?"

"No—he is well where he is. In the early days we buried our dead in a square box and we placed the box about a third of the way up a large tree, and we cut off the limbs below the box so the animals could not reach it, and later, other boxes were hauled up by ropes and each family had its own burial tree."

"I have seen them."

"Later we cut down a large tree ten feet from the ground and on its stump we built a house, and in the house we placed ten boxes and sometimes more."

"I have seen them also."

"But now many boxes have fallen from the trees and other trees have fallen on the grave houses built on the stumps. The bones of our ancestors lie scattered on the ground, and the old totems and the carvings are broken and beyond repair."

"If this disturbs you," Mark said, choosing his words carefully, "we can build a large communal grave and in it we can place all the boxes and the broken carvings. And if you wish in the morning I will go with you and the older men to start the clearing."

The old people rose.

"It is well," T. P. said. "I will stop by for you in the morning."

The next day the fine weather holding, Mark went with the elder men of the tribe, and what had seemed so reasonable a project became suddenly huge and macabre.

The little path that led to the ancient burial ground was overgrown. When they had cut their way through it, they saw that the year's windfall had been severe and that the old grave houses and the boxes that had fallen from the trees were covered with brush and branches.

For five days the men of the tribe worked at the clearing, and when this was done, Jim and other younger men went up the huge spruce trees with ropes to lower the grave boxes that were still intact. Where any box had fallen and touched the ground, only bones were left, but where the boxes had remained in the air, the bodies were partially mummified, the wrists still holding the copper bracelets, green now and paper-thin; and beside the heads were ancient water vessels placed there in case the soul of the dead thirsted on his journey.

When the huge grave was dug and ready, forty boxes were placed in it, and all the broken bones and bits of ancient grave posts and carvings. The men who had done the work buried also the clothes they had worn. Then on a sunny, clear morning, Mark held a brief service and the grave was covered. When it was over, he saw relief in the eyes of the old, and again T. P. spoke for them.

"At last a man has come to us who has seen to it that our dead can rest in peace."

When he returned along the little path to the village, Mark stopped at the house of Peter, the carver, and sat a moment on the steps to chat.

"When spring comes, grass will grow over the

huge new grave," Peter said. "The air will be sweet smelling again from the wild flowers, and the old people will walk there often."

"Why will they go there, Peter?" Mark asked slowly.

"To be sure that at last our dead are safe from the hamatsa."

"I do not know the myth of the hamatsa."

"The myth is a story. There is no harm in the myth, and I will tell it to you.

"A young man was ready to dance and he did not know what dance to do. He stood up in his red cedar bark dress, and he threw off his blankets, and he walked up a mountain until he came to a lake and saw a loon. The loon said, 'I know why you have come and I will help you,' and he led him to a house from which smoke came and told him to enter. The doorkeeper let him in and asked him to sit, and the second man, who was the cannibal man, asked why he had come, and the young man answered, 'Because I want to be as you are.'"

"And then?" Mark asked.

"And then the cannibal man went behind a screen and came out with a body, and he gobbled up one, and he gobbled two, and he gobbled up four, because that is the ceremonial number, and a lady followed him around and put the bones in a basket. Then he danced four times around the house and disappeared up a pole, and he put into the young man the whistle which makes the cannibal cry, and he tied hemlock branches to his wrists and ankles to protect him, and the young man did the dance as he had been shown, and returned to his village.

"And one night his people decided to give a dance. They lighted a pitch pole and sent four of the villagers to bring water, but none came back. They heard the hamatsa cry and recognized the young man, and they knew he had been bewitched by the cannibal man and had eaten the four people.

"They sang their songs and piled food boxes to the ceremonial house roof and the roof opened, and they heard a skull roll down its side, and were afraid.

"The next night his people tried to get the young man into the house to tame him, and he came four times on four nights, and they thought he was safely cured because he had fallen in love with a maiden. On the last night they knew he was not cured, so they killed him with magic, and he returned to the wood and was not seen again. And this is the myth which the old men tell and it is harmless."

"And the dance was based on the myth?"

"Yes. In the winter ceremonials, the hamatsa dance was the last and it took four nights. The young man who did it disappeared from the village and he lived beyond the old burial ground in a little cedar house hidden in the deep woods. I know, because when I was a young boy, my father's house was the last in the village, and I was the one who took him food.

"My friend, you cannot imagine what it was like—the tribe waiting on the first night of the dance, and the hamatsa coming at last, crying in the woods. In my father's day if anyone laughed, if he made a mistake in the dances, he was killed. In my father's day when the hamatsa entered on the second night of the dance carrying a real body taken from the old burial ground, the women were afraid, and they said, 'Is the body from my family's tree? Is it one of ours?' When I was a boy

the hamatsa carried no body because the government forbade it, and he only pretended to bite
people, holding a piece of seal liver in his mouth.
As a boy I saw the scars on the arms of the old
men, and I heard the tales."

Then Peter was silent, and Mark left him and
walked along down the path through the woods.

How had it been in the old days when the
magic, and supernatural spirits, and the cannibal
man who lived at the north end of the world had
dominated life here in this village? How had it
been when the hamatsa had come in the night
through the great trees, crying his soft and terri-
ble call? He would never know. No man would
ever know. But Mark had seen the light of the old,
old ways reflected on the faces like the glow from
a dying campfire, and he knew that it was the
hamatsa who had been freed at last from his holy
madness, and was at peace in the deep woods.

SIXTEEN

Fall came gently with the second blooming of the dogwood. No wind blew, the clouds hung low over the village, and the rains were soft. When Mark and Jim came home from patrol, Keetah was always waiting on the black sands, and Gordon's uncle also.

Had Caleb written? And how did it go with Gordon? Did he miss his village?

"Caleb has written and it does not go well. Gordon can't eat. He can't sleep. He is losing weight," and in the evening in the cedar houses along the path the old ones spoke the same words, softly and with hope. "He will come back to us as Jim came back. He is still an Indian."

Then Caleb's letters brightened. Gordon was studying hard and well. He planned to do two years' work in one. In the little cedar houses along the path, the old nodded their heads. "And by the end of the year, he will be cured of his madness and he will return to his people."

Slowly, as the needles fell, the waters of the inlet grew less clear, and on the river floated the first green leaves of the alders. When the nights cooled, the little berry bush burned crimson under the great, dark cedar, and on one deep green island side, a single cottonwood turned gold.

Now the land belonged first to the wild fowl. Coming up the inlet, Mark would stop the engine of the little boat to hear the loud calling of the first immense flocks of snow geese on their way from

Siberia to the Sacramento Valley. He knew the
white fronts that came from Bristol Bay, and
watched for the white markings on the dark necks
of the Canada geese. He knew the black brants
that fed late on the eel grass of Izemberg Bay,
passing high over the village like a long whisper,
like a sigh, on their way to Baja California.

Here every bird and fish knew its course. Every
tree had its own place upon this earth. Only man
had lost his way. Then, when the geese had
passed, and the bear and the little hibernating animals had hidden themselves for their long sleep,
the white trunks of the alders stood stripped and
stark across the river, and man began to emerge,
to prove again his capacity for endurance and
faithfulness. It was in loneliness the Indians had
lived through all the centuries, and it was in loneliness Mark came to know them best.

He relied on Jim as he had never relied on anyone, yet their friendship was forged in the long
hours on the boat in which neither spoke an un-
necessary word. And always there was the trip in
the little open boat up the cold river, and the
vicarage waiting with the warm food on the back
of the stove that Marta had placed there, the
clothes Keetah had washed and ironed, the wood
old Peter had cut and stacked, the piece of fish or
game set aside from each and every hunt. And
there were the Indians who dropped by in the
evening to offer help or ask it, and the children
who entered without knocking to stand, motionless, watching him from their big, soft eyes,
smiling shyly.

Thus fall flowed past the village like the river,
and again Mark stood in the small hushed church
on Christmas Eve with the candlelight glowing on
the golden eagle, watching the lights go out, and

his people coming down the path through the trees. When he opened the door to meet them, he saw that Gordon had come home to his village.

He saw Gordon with a surge of pride and a twinge of anguish. Gone was the shy and eager boy in the fisherman's trousers and jacket, the dark hair a little long on the neck. How much he had changed and how fast—a handsome young man in his city suit, his white shirt and tie, and on his face the discipline that marked the size of his battle.

When he came up the steps with Keetah, Mark held out his hand and said, "Welcome home, Gordon. And how does it go with you?" and Gordon answered gravely, "It goes well, Mark. Thank you," and he shook hands as does the white man.

Now the wind of unease was again in the village—even here in the church. When T. P., Gordon's grandfather, came to the rail and held up his hands for the bread from the paten, Mark saw that the fine old man could not keep them from trembling.

Each day Mark and Jim set out early to take Christmas to the hand-logger and his family, to Calamity Bill, and the remote camps, and to the other villages. Each time they returned, the village was full of mutterings:

"Gordon does not even look like an Indian. Have you not noticed?"

"He does not dip his fish into the gleena. He speaks down to us. He is critical of ways he has known all his life."

"That is natural. One must expect it. He will finish his year at school and return to stay. He will return as Jim came back to us, and he will let his hair grow and put on his old clothes, and he will be one of us, and free."

One evening there was a knock at the vicarage and when Mark answered the door, Gordon's grandfather and uncle waited in the dark. He asked them to come in and to be seated. When they had done so, it was the grandfather who spoke.

"We are having a family dinner for Gordon. Since we know that on the night it is to be held you will be on patrol, we have come to tell you of our plans for him."

"I can tell you some of the plans, T. P. I have seen the change in him as you have seen it, and I have tried to stand in your shoes. When he returns in the summer you will give a great potlatch and at it you will give him the ceremonial rites of your family, and the dances that have come down in it."

"Yes, that is part of it. When the rains have ceased, the men of the family will build his house, and when he and Keetah are married, we will give them a fine wedding with the canoes moving up and down the river bringing the guests, and all the houses of the village filled, and a great wedding feast."

And the uncle said quickly, "And next year I shall remain in the village during the fishing. Gordon will be in charge of the gill-netter. When the run is good, he will make as much as four thousand dollars in the season. No young man in the village will have so fine a future."

The old man leaned forward.

"Mark, will you urge him to agree?"

"No, I will not. This is something he must decide. I am sure he knows it now, because he is avoiding me. If he comes back to stay, I shall be proud of him. If he decides to remain outside, although it breaks your hearts, in the end you will be proud of him also."

Mark and Jim were at another village on the night the dinner was given for Gordon. Neither mentioned it, nor forgot it. In his mind Mark could see them, the old and middle-aged of the family clan, gathered in T. P.'s old cedar house beneath the dark trees, and he could see T. P. making his appeal in the ancient Kwákwala, the others listening, waiting for Gordon's answer.

A gale delayed their return. When at last they came up the river in the gray rain, the village was still. Not an Indian was visible. When they entered the vicarage, no child came to welcome them. They knew now Gordon's answer.

He came after dark. With him was Keetah.

"You have decided?" Mark asked.

"Yes. I asked time to consider, and for two days and nights I have thought of nothing else. But that is not why I have come. I have come to ask if you will take me to Alert Bay in the morning where I can get the plane?"

"Of course. You know I will."

"Then I will go now and tell my grandfather I want to remain outside, that I want to go to the university. I want to be the first of my people to enter a profession. When I left here it was like taking a knife and cutting a piece out of myself, but to tell my grandfather I do not wish to come back to stay—this is to take a knife and cut through the flesh and bone of my own people."

"I know."

"Mark, I cannot come home again. I have changed too much. It is my mind that has changed. I can never come home again."

"Someday you will be able to live in both

worlds. And I will tell you something, Gordon, as I told your grandfather. You will represent your people in the outside world and they will be proud of you. And even if you cannot return, you will find that the work you do, the kind of man you are, all that is deepest and best in you will be based on what you have learned here. And one more thing. Tell me—what of Keetah?"

"She will go with me. I can't leave her. She will go with me. She does not promise to stay, but she will try."

Early the next morning before dawn the four went down the river to the float. When they left on the larger boat, Gordon remained on the aft deck in the cold rain, looking up at the mountains and the steep green sides of the inlet. Keetah said good-bye to nothing. She made coffee and carried the mugs into the cabin for Mark and Jim. Not once did she look directly at either.

When they reached Alert Bay, there was only time to catch the seaplane and for a hasty handshake. When Mark and Jim returned to the boat to start home, it was Jim who spoke first.

"Keetah will come back. She knows it now."

"Gordon will do well, and in the end he will be able to live in both worlds," Mark said. "But if Keetah is not strong enough to return by choice and not by failure, she will never again be able to live in either."

SEVENTEEN

Shortly after Christmas the hospital ship arrived on patrol. When Mark heard the put-put of the small boat bringing the doctor and the captain to the village, he went to the river's edge to meet them and saw to his delight that Caleb had come also.

"I invited myself," announced Caleb. "I hitched a ride, and do you know what these sinners did? They passed a resolution behind my back that any guest who complained about the food should be automatically elected cook. Then they served me the worst lunch I ever ate in my life. Lad, save me. I have peeled spuds up the Johnstone Straits," and Mark said he could stay as long as he wished and not a spud in sight.

Again the kitchen was turned into a clinic. When the pills had been dispensed, the children given their shots, and the teeth pulled, word came from Village island that an Indian had broken his leg, and the doctor and captain left hastily. Mark cleaned up the kitchen and put on the coffee pot. He told Caleb of Gordon and Keetah, but the old priest made no comment, and Mark sensed he had come for some specific reason. But for what? Did he think Mark had not done well? Was that it?

Outside dusk was coming, and a cold rain fell.

"I like the rain, lad. Surely it was on the bleak and rainy nights that the coastal Indians began to create an identity for themselves. There were perhaps eighty thousand in all, speaking many dialects, belonging to many tribes, scattered in many small villages over a very long and intricate coast line. Yet they began in the same way, as we began."

"With the myths, Caleb?"

"Yes. They hunted the sea, and the sea teemed with fish, the woods were full of game and berries, and the air with fowl. Food was easy to find. This gave them time to create, and they shared one splendid friend."

"What?"

"The cedar tree. It had a thick brown pelt from which they could make clothes and blankets. It split readily under their first stone axes and wooden wedges. They made their houses and canoes from cedar. They carved masks and totems from its wood. In gratitude they turned it into a myth, and if you look out the window into the rain, you will see the Cedar-man at the bottom of the great totem holding up the crests of this tribe."

Mark refilled the coffee cups.

"Three summers ago I flew to the Queen Charlottes," Caleb said slowly. "An old Haida friend met me with his boat, and we spent several days visiting the ancient deserted Haida villages, even Tanu, the most famous of them all.

"The one I remember best had no name. It did not even exist in memory. No one knew how long it had been deserted or why. We moored the boat and rowed ashore. One totem faced the beach, gray and simple as a Greek column. But in the deep woods we found what was left of several others, badly broken and covered with moss, new trees growing from their ruin. They had come

from the forest, and the forest had reclaimed
them.

"And suddenly the place became eerie, as if
eyes were watching us, the silence filled with
voices we felt but couldn't hear. We were in-
truders and we knew it, and walked quickly to the
beach and rowed to the boat, and we did not look
back."

"Caleb, why are you telling me this?"

"Because it is going to happen to Kingcome and
sooner than we think. The long trek down the
lonely coast is not yet over. The young will follow
Gordon. Very soon only the old will be left and a
very few others, and when the old die, the others
will leave. The tribe is going to trade its simplicity
for the shiny gadgetry of our complex world, and
it will not be so content, because there is one
thing it does not anticipate. The outside world
will not accept it easily."

There was a long silence.

"And now it's my turn, Caleb," said Mark.
"You're right. In the end they will all leave, and
the wrong people will use them for the wrong rea-
sons. For publicity, for politics, for egotism, even
for greed. But you have forgotten something.
They have one splendid friend who understands
them and will stand by them. They have men like
you, Caleb. Don't you know yet that in life you
have been to this tribe what the Cedar-man was to
them in the myth?"

The old priest looked abashed.

"I hope it's a little bit true, Mark," he said hum-
bly. "And if it is true of me, it is true of you also."

PART FOUR

Come wolf,
come swimmer

EIGHTEEN

One afternoon in January the weather turned very cold, and on the river in any little protected spot where the current was not so swift, ice began to form. For two days all the able men of the tribe broke ice in a desperate attempt to keep the river free that the boats might move, but on the third night Mark, who had taken his turn, awoke to the sound of the canoes being dragged up on the bank, and he arose and made a huge pot of coffee to take to them.

The next morning the children were walking gleefully across the river on the firm ice, and by afternoon the men were walking across also to drag any wood that would burn, because now the village was ice-bound and no boat could go for oil, or propane.

To keep fed, to keep warm, to keep alive. No woman said, "I am sorry. I have only enough fuel for my own family," and no man said, "It is true that I have shot a deer. I am freezing what I do not need now. I cannot share with you, friend."

Then huge wet flakes fell in place of the dry snow and ice began to break in the river, and Mark and Jim reached the float by canoe, and went by boat to the float store to bring back food and forty-five gallon drums of oil and one hundred pound tanks of propane.

Men of the tribe met them at the float to help load the canoes, the snow still falling heavily, the mountains and the sides of the inlet ghostly white in the night. And it seemed to Mark that the river was life itself, flowing by the village with all its wonder and its agony.

When the cold rain replaced the snow, there was illness in the village. Twice the hospital ship reached the float, and Jim and Mark brought the doctor by canoe to the village. The kitchen of the vicarage became a clinic, and the doctor trudged down the wet soggy paths visiting those too old, or too sick to come to him. And twice an elder was wrapped in blankets, and carried in the bottom of a canoe in a heavy rain to the hospital boat and on to Alert Bay. But nobody died.

In February the clamming at Gilford began, and for the first time in six weeks Mark reached the other villages of his patrol. In the log book he wrote "full gale" again and again, hiding out the storms in some little cove on the leeward side of an island. And when he reached the small villages, the little portable altar was set up in the school house or a private dwelling, a hymn or two sung with someone playing the accordion, or the banjo. It was always the same. It was not fine sermons they sought now in the long cruel winter. It was communion.

Mark and Jim spent five days in the other villages and on the way home, when they went through Whale Pass and could see the white Kingcome Mountains, they passed the A-frame on Calamity's float, and, as he always did, Mark looked to see if smoke was coming from Calamity's little shack. None was.

"He's probably away," Jim said. "All the big camps are still closed because of snow. Nothing but a skeleton crew left anywhere. I expect some logging boat stopped and took him out."

"Pull up alongside, Jim. I'd better check."

How many times he had stopped to hide out a gale or to chart, and always Calamity had taken out the carved walrus tusk which was the cribbage board, and always he had said, "Just one game, Mark, while I put on a mite of supper."

But this time when he knocked at the door, no rough voice answered him, and he opened the door and stepped in. There was the table with its ancient oil cloth cover, and the coffee pot, doubtless half full of grounds, waiting for Calamity to toss in a handful of coffee and boil it up again. There was the broken easy chair, and on the cot in the corner lay Calamity.

Mark pulled the chair close to the cot and sat down, and he reached over and touched the shoulder.

"What's the matter, old-timer? Did you get hit by a widow-maker?"

"I knew you'd come, lad. I been waiting. I went upside to check the snow and damned if I didn't slip off the cliff and wake up with the tide lickin' at my boots. Had to drag myself to the shack."

"How long have you been here?"

"Four days, maybe. All I need is some food within reach and the stove going, and I'd take it kindly if you'd move the cot so I can put in a stick now and then."

Mark went over him carefully.

"I think you've broken a hip, Calamity. What you need is a trip to Alert Bay. If the hospital ship's close enough, she'll take you, and if she's too far to get here, I'll take you."

"Damn waste of money. First thing they'd do is take off my red long-johns and I'd die of pneumonia." And Mark asked of himself, "And what do you think you're doing now?"

While Mark built the fire, Jim sent out an emergency on the radio-telephone, but the hospital ship was too far away to come and the gale warnings were out and the straits too rough to cross. But it didn't matter. It was too late for help and Mark knew it, and Calamity knew it also.

Mark sat beside the cot.

"I ain't much of a church man, Mark. Guess you might say I'm an agnostic. I don't know."

"There's a good bit of agnostic in all of us, Calamity. None of us knows much—only enough to trust to reach out a hand in the dark."

"Under my pillow there's a map of Knight's Inlet. I put a cross on the place where I cut trees once. I always thought that when it was my time to conk out, I'd kind of like my ashes—"

"I'll do it, Calamity. It's a promise."

"Don't say no fine words about me; we'll both know they're lies. Do it in the spring, on some fine day."

Mark sat by Calamity through the deep night, until the hand he held slipped from his, and the period between breaths grew longer and longer. At dawn the old hand-logger sighed deeply and was done. Then Mark covered the body with a blanket and returned to the boat to catch the first weather report, which promised that by noon the straits might be navigable. By radio-telephone he managed at last to reach his friend, the sergeant, and tell him what had happened, and ask permission to bring the body of Calamity for cremation, and this he was given. Then he lay down for a few hours' sleep.

When he awakened and went out on the deck to check, the weather had improved somewhat. He stepped again into one of those small unforgettable events he had come to expect. The skeletal crew in the nearest camp had picked up the news of Calamity's death on the radio-tele-phone and, feeling it unseemly that he go on his last journey tied in an old tarpaulin, they had put together a proper box to hold him.

There were six men in all in two small boats, and a third boat bringing the couple from the float store, who had picked up the news also and come to help, the wife with an old suit of her hus-band's folded over the arm because she was sure that at last she was going to part Calamity from his red long-johns and send him to his Maker suit-ably garbed. But when Mark and Jim had caught the lines and she held out the suit without a word, Mark shook his head.

"Calamity wouldn't be separated from them in life," he said gently, "and I don't think he'd want to change now," and for an instant a bit of laugh-ter rose in the solemn eyes beneath the knit caps in all the toughened faces, and was instantly squelched.

Two of the loggers helped put Calamity in the box, and carry it to the aft of the boat, and lash it down. Then Mark put on his cassock and said for Calamity a few very simple prayers. After the blessing Jim struck eight bells to mark the end of the watch and loosed the line, and Calamity start-ed his last rough journey to what he had always called the happy logging country.

When they had moved well out from the float where the last of a southwesterly funneled up the inlet, Mark looked back to see the small group still standing on the little float on the snowy inlet side.

He never passed the float on patrol that he did not say a small prayer for the old-timer and remember his promise.

"In the spring, Calamity. On the first fine day."

NINETEEN

In the long winter no one asked, "How does it go with Keetah?" One afternoon when Mark stopped at Marta's house on some small errand, he found her sitting by her fire, knitting a heavy gray Indian sweater, a polar bear in white on the back, and he asked, "Is it for me?" and Marta answered, "Not this time. It is for Keetah."

"You think she will return?"

"Yes."

"By choice, and not by defeat?"

"Yes, Mark, by choice," and Marta's soft dark eyes searched his long and carefully, and she said no more.

Keetah returned on a windy, bleak March day. She flew to Gilford village and one of the tribe, returning to Kingcome for the week-end from the clamming, brought her to the float.

She came up the river sitting very straight on the narrow crosspiece of the canoe, and when it reached the beach in front of the vicarage, she did not let the men carry her to the bank. She took off her city shoes, stepped out into the cold water and waded ashore, standing motionless on the black sands of her village, turning slowly to look at Whoop-Szo rising across the river, at Kingcome Mountains back of the village.

From the vicarage, Mark heard the smaller children run to greet her, and Marta also, and he went to the window to watch, and he knew Keetah was no longer the shy, sweet, young girl who had wept at the end of the swimmer. Keetah had returned a woman.

That evening Mark waited in the vicarage for Keetah's knock, sure she would come to tell him of Gordon, of Caleb, of all that had happened to her in the great outside world. She did not come; no one knocked on the vicarage door, and the next day he saw her only at a distance.

On Sunday morning Keetah was in her usual place, but when the service was over and Mark stood at the door shaking each hand, "And how was the clamming at Gilford?"—"And has the part for your boat come yet, Sam?"—she slipped away without a word.

He waited and asked no questions, not even of Jim. For the first time since the death of the woman by breech birth, it seemed to him that again the dark eyes watched him cautiously. Keetah had returned to her people, and they knew why and accepted her as if she had not been away, but would he? It was Mark they doubted and he realized, suddenly, even yet he did not know them—perhaps no white man would ever know them—and he knew they knew him better than he did himself.

On Saturday morning two weeks after Keetah's return, Mark carried a load of firewood to the church as was his custom, and when he had placed it in the wood box, he turned to see Keetah standing quietly by the golden eagle, and he went to her slowly and held out his hands.

"I knew you'd come. You have been afraid I would not approve because you have returned to the village. Is that not it? Oh, Keetah, do you trust me so little?" And he sat down in the first pew and she beside him, but it was a long time before she spoke.

Caleb had been kind to her. Everyone had been kind to her. Caleb had found her a place to live, and work for her board and room while she went to school. The woman of the house had been afraid at first because she had never known an Indian girl, and she had asked, "Is she dirty? Will she steal?" and the woman had spoken to her as if she were a child. "You must take two baths a week. You must be in the house every night by half-past seven," though the woman had never helped with birth or death, and would have been afraid to do so. At school she had not belonged. She was older than the others, and the two younger Indian girls had said to her, "What is this old one doing here?"

Keetah spoke haltingly, never once lifting her eyes. Then she stood up slowly, and Mark also.

"I could not sleep. I could not eat. I missed my village. I missed my gleena and my fish dishes. At night I dreamed of the black sands of Kingcome and of the mountains. The world swallowed me, and I knew I could not stay there because my village is the only place I know myself."

"The world is here also, Keetah."

"Each day I saw my Gordon grow more and more like the white man until even in church the white girls said, 'Who is that good-looking boy?' I am too Indian for Gordon now and I know it and he knows it. He will marry a white girl who can do more for him than I can do, or he will marry an Indian girl who has lived outside since she was very small. I lost my sister to death. I have lost Gordon to life, and this is harder. But there is something harder yet."

"To come home, Keetah?"

"Yes, to come home to the village I love. It is the same. I am not. I have seen how the white man treats his woman. He shares his pleasures and even his work. He does not marry her and leave her to fish. Now I know what Gordon knew long ago. To be an Indian in my own village is to be free as no white man is ever free, and it is to live behind a wall. I did not tell Gordon I was returning, but I think he knew. Sometimes, when he was not working at his books, we walked away from the town through the trees and into the woods. I stayed until I was sure that when I came home I would bear his child."

"To hold him—to make him marry you—to force him to return?"

"No! He does not know. He will not return for many years, and when he does, no one will tell him. Not to hold him. To let him go. To keep a part of him here in his village with his own people so they can last, so I too, can live."

Then she waited, her eyes fixed on his.

What she had done was logical to her, and if he told her it was wrong, he would destroy her.

"What you have done is strange to me, but I think I understand it. You will grow over the wall. You will remain as long as the village lasts, and someday you will take Marta's place and become one of the great women of your tribe, and I shall always be proud of you."

That night, over supper, Mark said to Jim, "Keetah is going to have Gordon's child. Did you know?"

"Yes."

"And does this change you?"

"A child is always welcome," Jim said. "When I marry her, her child will be mine."

TWENTY

On a Sunday in late March there occurred another of those small unforgettable happenings Mark had grown to expect. The snow was gone. Day after day the rain had fallen patiently. When Mark shook up the fire in the big round stove and rang the church bell, he noticed that the leaden sky, which had overhung the village all winter long, seemed less dark and gloomy. During the communion service, just as he spoke the old, old words, "Therefore, with Angels and Archangels and with all the company of heaven," bright light suddenly filled the church and all the bowed heads lifted to see the sun glistening on the snows that crowned Whoop-Szo, and it seemed to Mark that he felt the burden of the winter lift as from a common shoulder, and heard the sigh of gratitude rise from a common heart.

When the service was over, the tribe poured slowly from the church, lingering in little groups on the path by the Cedar-man at the foot of the great totem.

"How thin we are," said old Peter. "We are like the bear when he leaves his den, and stands blinking in the light."

They all agreed, nodding that the cruel winter had been hard on them all. Then T. P., the elder, grandfather of Gordon, went up the steps of the church, lifted his arm and cried, "Quiet. Be still. I have something to say of importance. When the clamming is done, and the fishing has not yet begun, while we are waiting for the óolachon, I am giving a dance-potlatch for Jim, my grand-nephew, to pass to him the rights, the ceremonies of my family. All our tribe is invited and our rela-tives in the other villages, and there will be a feast and gifts for all."

One of the older men, distantly related, climbed the steps also to stand beside the old man, and he said to T. P.: "If it is pleasing to you, my branch of the family will give a feast also in honour of your family, and we will dance in honour of your nephew."

"It will please me."

Now everyone began to laugh and to talk in Kwákwala, the young women drawing around Mrs. Hudson, who would undoubtedly be asked to estimate the food which must be brought in by boat and to help choose the gifts. The younger men formed another group, and the older men a third.

"We will have at least three hundred people in the village. How will we feed them . . . ?"

"Let us do the Dog Dance. Let us do dances that were created here in our own village."

"Then we must check the masks. We must make sure the strings work properly so the fins of the fish can move and the mouths open."

Under a green spruce Marta stood by herself, her eyes on the young vicar. How thin and white he was! How long had it been there—that look on his face she had seen many times in her long life and knew well? It was not the hard winter that had placed it there. It was death reaching out his hand, touching the face gently, even before the owl had called the name.

While the others were still talking of the pot-latch, Marta returned to her house and slowly,

and with much care, she wrote a letter to the
Bishop:

"My lord, it is your friend, Marta Stephens,
who keeps her promise now. When T. P., the elder, gives a potlatch for Jim Wallace you come. It
is time you come then. God bless you."

For three weeks the village was busier than
Mark had ever seen it, except during the building
of the new vicarage. At night in the social hall the
older men checked the masks. After school the
children practised the dance steps at their play.
The younger men cleaned the big house, built
plank seats for the visitors who had been asked,
and gathered wood for the great fire which would
burn in the middle of the dirt floor.

Mrs. Hudson checked the ceremonial robes to
be sure the abalone shells and the ancient buttons
were still sewed tight, and she and the women of
Jim and Gordon's families made two trips to Alert
Bay for the gifts and food.

At last all was ready. The gill-netters and the
seiners began to arrive at the float from the other
villages, and hour after hour the canoes moved up
and down the river bringing the guests. When the
last canoe arrived two of the Indians stepped into
the cold water in their Kingcome slippers and carried the Bishop ashore and a little whisper of ex-
citement ran through the spruce, as the children
spread the news. "The Bissop is here. The Bissop
has come."

That night there was a great feast in the social
hall. Then the tribe walked to the big house where
T. P. and his family greeted the guests and seated
them. Then there was nothing in all the world but
the shadows of the carved house posts, the swirl-
ing ermine-tailed robes, the flickering of the great
fire; no sound but the beat of the drums, the

rhythm of the rattles, the chanting of the songs. Mark and the Bishop sat to the right of the fire in the place of honour, and saw the dance of the fish and the dog dance. They saw Jim do the dance of the angry man lost in the woods; his bird mask was so big that another dancer had to guide him lest he fall in the fire. It was all that was left of the famous hamatsa.

At dawn when the dancing was done and the guests served refreshments, gifts of linen, towels and shirts were distributed, and at the end as the guests left, each was handed a bright silver dollar.

On the second day there was another great feast and more dancing, and on the third morning the exodus began. When the canoes had taken the last guests down the river, the Bishop lingered in the quiet village. Once Mark saw him talking to Marta by the river's edge. When he walked to the end of the village on an errand, he saw the Bishop sitting with Peter, the carver, on the porch of the last house. In the late afternoon he saw him go into the church by himself.

"Something worries him. He has taken his problem into the church as I have done so many times, and put it down at the altar."

At dinner in the vicarage, the Bishop spoke little, and early the next morning the two of them left the village in the speed boat to go to the float.

When they entered the inlet, the Bishop motioned Mark to stop the engine.

"Let's not hurry," he said. "It's so seldom I have a few hours to myself."

The breeze was gentle with the first promise of spring. They could see the float moored to the inlet side and beyond it they could see the jagged scar of the great slide.

"Always when I leave the village," the Bishop said slowly, "I try to define what it means to me, why it sends me back to the world refreshed and confident. Always I fail. It is so simple, it is difficult. When I try to put it into words, it comes out one of those unctuous, over-pious platitudes at which Bishops are expected to excel."

They both laughed.

"But when I reach here and see the great scar where the inlet side shows its bones, for a moment I know."

"What, my lord?"

"That for me it has always been easier here, where only the fundamentals count, to learn what every man must learn in this world."

"And that, my lord?"

"Enough of the meaning of life to be ready to die," and the Bishop motioned Mark to start the motor, and they went on.

On the three-hour trip to the float store, they took turns at the wheel. Once the Bishop left the cabin and Mark could hear him in the galley banging the pots and pans. When he returned he carried a plate of sandwiches and two mugs of coffee. When they came at last to the store, the two raccoons greeted them with their strange whirring sound, and the Bishop fed them the crusts.

It was not until the seaplane set down on the water that the Bishop spoke.

"I will begin at once to seek a replacement for you, Mark. Your work in the village is almost done. When I have found the right man to take your place, I shall write you, and when you come out, you will come to me."

"Yes, my lord."

TWENTY-ONE

When the little seaplane lifted and was gone, Mark turned back to his boat, checked the oil and water, and started to Knight's Inlet to keep his promise to Calamity Bill. Already nothing looked the same because it was going to end, because he was going to leave it, and the thought filled him with a twinge of sudden anguish and the little, unexpected fear that precedes any big change, sad or joyous.

How would he live again in the old world he had almost forgotten, where men throw up smoke screens between themselves and the fundamentals whose existence they fear but seldom admit? Here, where death waited behind each tree, he had made friends with loneliness, with death and deprivation, and, solidly against his back had stood the wall of his faith.

How much had he accomplished? If he asked him, he knew what the Bishop's answer would be: "You may never know, or perhaps something you have done will reveal itself in Keetah's child, in Gordon's life. You have done your small bit."

And what had he learned? Surely not the truth of the Indian. There was no one truth. He had learned a little of the truth of one tribe in one village. He had seen the sadness, the richness, the tragic poignancy of a way of life that each year, bit by bit, slipped beyond memory and was gone. For a time he had been part of it, one of the small unknown men who take their stand in some remote place, and fight out their battle in a quiet way.

When Mark was well into Knight's Inlet, he came on a strange sight. Two loggers were moving their float camp to a new location. The dwelling houses, the machine shop, the garden and the loading floats, made a double row, all enclosed by boom-sticks, joined end to end with chains. A tug boat had attached its towing cable to the gill-poke at the end of the A-frame float, and was pulling valiantly.

But the tide was running, and when Mark slowed his boat and drew as close to the tug as he dared, he was sure that the little community was scarcely moving at all, and he opened the cabin door and hailed them.

"How're you doing?" and the tug boat captain yelled back they'd made twenty-five miles in twenty-three hours, and four more to go, and Mark yelled back that he'd help with the tow.

He stayed with the haul for six hours, sometimes at the wheel of his own boat, when a man from the tug relieved him, in one of the dwelling houses on the floats. The Scottish granny of the two brothers who owned the camp made sandwiches and a pot of tea. The three children showed him the tiny schoolroom where, every morning, Granny taught them. The two wives showed him the light plant, the washing machine, the refrigerator.

The smaller girl put in his lap Robert Burns, the tomcat, respected by all because last summer when a large brown bear had walked a boom log onto the dwelling float, he had greeted him with such an outraged screech that the bear had fallen off the log and into the chuck.

The float camp seemed to stand still, while the

green sides of the inlet moved by, slowly and ma-
jestically. When the new site was reached and the
boats stopped, the two loggers discussed with him
for a bit the new logging methods, the greater
number of logs, the higher costs. When he left
them, these staunch and kindly people, he felt
somehow that he had known them all his life.

Now, beside the compass, he placed the map he
had taken from under Calamity's pillow, watching for the narrow finger of the sea on the left
side of the inlet, found and entered it, slowing
the boat until it barely moved, seeking the cove
Calamity had marked with a cross. When he saw
it, he stopped the engine and let the boat drift
slowly in.

At flood tide no eddy moved, no ripple marred
the surface. On the water Mark saw reflected the
cliffs that rose above the narrow fingerling, the
green spruce and cedar, and one huge hemlock
that must have been growing when Christ was a
little lad. Here he gave the ashes of Calamity to
the sea, and when he came to the last words of
the committal, "Rest eternal grant unto him, O
Lord," he heard the echo of the words come back
to him from across the narrow channel, softly
and eerily, as if from another world. Then there
was no sound but the soft mewing of the gulls
nesting in the cliffs.

"Calamity, my friend," he thought, "you have
had a funeral finer than a king's and this is the
way it ought to be, and I have seen it once," and
he started the engine and went on up the fingerling to its end and anchored there for the night.

In the morning after breakfast, he started back
to the village, and when he passed the site where
he had left the float camp, he sounded the whistle
and the Scottish granny and the children rushed

out of the house to wave and call to him. After that he saw no one; he passed no boat.

All day long he moved down the longest, the loveliest of all the inlets, and it seemed to him that something strange had happened to time. When he had first come to the village, it was the future that loomed huge. So much to plan. So much to learn. Then it was the present that had consumed him—each day with all its chores and never enough hours to do them. Now time had lost its contours. He seemed to see it as the raven or the bald eagle, flying high over the village, must see the part of the river that had passed the village, that had not yet reached the village, one and the same.

All day long, on his way back to Kingcome, because he was alone and receptive, the little questions, the observations he had pushed deep within him, began to rise slowly toward the door of the conscious mind which was almost ready to open, to receive them, and give them words: "You are tired. You have told yourself that it was due to the winter which was hard on everyone. Deep inside haven't you known it was more than this? When the Bishop came to the potlatch and lingered after the others had gone, and went into the church by himself, didn't you guess then it had something to do with you? And your sister? When you took the boys down and lunched with her, did you not see the sadness in her eyes? And in the hospital, don't you remember the doctor's face, the look of quiet resignation upon it, and the way he hesitated an instant before answering your questions? And when the Bishop first told you of the village, how carefully he did so. Did you not think, "He is anxious I go there. Why?"

It was dusk when he entered Kingcome Inlet

and moored the boat at the float, and climbed into the speed boat. When he entered the river, the stars were shining, the moon bright also, and he went slowly.

Soon the huge flights of snow geese would fly over the river on their way back to the nesting place, the spring swimmer would come up the river to the Clearwater, and on the river pairs of cocky, small, red-necked sawbills would rest, the father flying off when Mark passed and the mother pretending she had broken a wing to lead him away from her little ones. And each would feel the pull of the earth and know his small place upon it, as did the Indian in his village.

He went slowly up the river. In front of the vicarage he anchored the boat and waded ashore. He trudged up the black sands to the path and stopped. From the dark spruce he heard an owl call—once, and again—and the questions that had been rising all day long reached the door of his mind and opened it.

He went up the path and the steps, through the living room and into the kitchen. The lights were on. At the stove Marta was preparing his dinner.

"Marta, something strange happened tonight. On the bank of the river I heard the owl call my name," and it was a question he asked, an answer he sought.

She did not say, "Nonsense, it was my name the owl called, and I am old and with me it does not matter." She did not say, "It's true you're thin and white, but who is not? It has no importance."

She turned, spoon still in her hand, lifting her sweet, kind face with its network of tiny wrinkles, and she answered his question as she would have answered any other.

She said, "Yes, my son."

TWENTY-TWO

In the night the heaviest of the spring rains fell in torrents as the young vicar struggled with the one fact of his life about which no man has doubt and yet is never ready to meet. One of the thoughts that comforted him was from his life here on the up-coast, the simple memory of the many times on the boat when he and Jim had seemed to be heading straight into a cliff or a steep island side only to find at the last moment some little finger of the sea waiting to lead them on. But almost as big as the fact of death was the thought of leaving. How could he return now to that far country he no longer knew, where, while awaiting death, he would be a stranger?

In the morning the rain had stopped, and the gray sky was broken by sun shining through soft white clouds. In the alders called the ravens, high over the river flew a flock of small birds he had come to know. As yearlings they had passed over the village in the fall, crossing lands they had never seen and with no older bird to guide them. Yet they had known their way to the southern valley where their kind had wintered for untold centuries, as now they knew their way back to the nesting place.

He walked slowly to the river bank. All was the same. The children too small to be in school came running to greet him. The older men were emptying rain water from the canoes, and Mrs. Hudson was poling out into the current to dump her garbage. The dark eyes held their usual sadness, the voices gentle, the mouths quick to smile, the hands lifting in the usual greeting.

"Good morning, Mark."

"What a rain we had. Did you hear it?"

"The village has become a sponge."

"But the morning will be splendid."

"It will not last. We will have another storm by night."

They did not know, and how could he tell them? How could he face the pity that would come to the sad eyes? And he tried desperately to speak as usual, and he turned slowly away and walked past the vicarage, and the church, past the Cedar-man at the foot of the great totem, following the main path through the quiet village. When he had passed the last house, which was that of Peter, the carver, he took the little narrow path through the deep wet woods, fragrant from rain, to the glade that was once the old burial ground.

There he stood alone in a world that had become a waiting room, and when he turned at last, he saw Keetah watching him. She came to him slowly and put her hands on his shoulders.

"I have come to speak for my people, Mark. There is something we wish you to do for us."

"But of course, Keetah. Anything I am able to do, I will do gladly."

"Stay with us. Marta has told us. We have written the Bishop and asked that he let you remain here to the end, because this is your village and we are your family. You are the swimmer who came to us from the great sea," and he put his arms around her and held her close, finding no

words to say thank you for the sudden, unexpected gift of peace which they had offered him in
their quiet, perceptive way.

In the late afternoon of this day there occurred
one of those minor emergencies typical of Mark's
life in the village. A young logger, long in the
woods, reached the beer parlour at a float store,
drank too much, too fast, stole a small motor
boat, and headed happily for the straits, despite
gale warnings, and predictions of a storm by
nightfall. Since his boat was the fastest, Mark
was summoned to aid in the search.

Jim received the message by radio-telephone on
the boat and came for Mark at once, and together
they went downriver, past the snags and the log
jam, and transferred to the larger boat at the
float. They went out the inlet, Jim at the wheel,
Mark perched on the stool, binoculars in hand,
ready to search the rocks, the reefs, the hidden
coves.

In two hours they had not found the drunken
logger. When they reached the place where the
boat began to pitch in the tidal sweep that came
down from Queen Charlotte Sound, they received
word by the radio-telephone that the young logger
had been found peacefully sleeping it off, his boat
neatly stuck between two rocks not three miles
from the float store from which he had started.

"And here we are in the cold, wasting oil, and
supperless," Jim said. "I hope he has the good
grace to drown himself."

"He won't even have a sniffle in his nose. I'll
make us some coffee."

They went back in silence, as they had so many
times. When they entered Kingcome Inlet, Mark
was at the wheel, Jim beside him watching for

drift logs in the searchlight.

"Jim."

"Yes."

"When I am no longer in the village, take care of Keetah. When you want coffee, don't bang on the table. Say *please* and when she hands you the cup, say *thank you*. You'll find it most efficacious."

"What is this *efficacious*?"

"It means it works. And when you build Keetah a house, let her plan it with you. And don't leave her alone in the village too long. Take her and the children with you sometimes on the fishing, and each year take her outside until it is familiar to her. Someday, when the village is no more, you too must cross the bridge."

"You ask me to do this for Keetah? Why?"

"Because I care for her also—and for you."

Then neither spoke, the wake from the bow white in the night. As they neared the float thunder sounded overhead, and lightning cut the sky and struck a tree at the top of the inlet forty yards ahead of the boat and high above them. The tree fell upon the trees below and, weakened by the heavy rains, they fell also, slowly at first, then faster and faster, end over end, until a long jagged strip peeled from the inlet side, and the whole world exploded into sound.

TWENTY-THREE

In the village the tribe heard the roar of the slide, prolonged and intensified as it was tossed from one steep inlet side to another until, even after the last of the trees had fallen and the waters begun to calm, the echoes still rumbled in the far distance, growing slowly fainter until they too were gone.

The tribe heard it and knew what it meant as had their ancestors. The sound lay in the oldest, deepest memories and in the myths. The sound was in the name of Whoop-Szo; "and the gods that lived on Noisy Mountain saw the enemy coming down the river and sent a huge slide to destroy it."

In the little cedar houses the men did not wait to light the lamps, but pulled on their shirts and trousers, their jackets and gum boots, seeking their tools and their lanterns. Footfalls sounded softly on the path that led past the dark vicarage to the river bank in a night suddenly starkly still. The water splashed as the men waded to the boats, a woman's voice following them, "Be careful—be careful," and the outboard motors sputtered and caught.

Then they were gone. The women were alone with the young, the old, the sick, as women have been left to wait through all the ages everywhere.

All night long the women waited. In the morning of the next day one of the men returned to bring news and take back food. The boat of the vicar had been caught in the slide and its wreckage sighted, and from the wreckage they had heard a voice call but they could not draw close enough to identify it. The RCMP had been summoned, the Bishop notified. The logging camps had sent men and boats to help.

All day long the women waited. But Keetah could not wait quietly with the others. When the bluejay called its name, "Kwiss-kwiss-kwiss-kwiss," it seemed to ask, "Which one? Which one?" and Keetah went through the village, through the dark, wet trees to the slope of the mountain that rose back of the village, and she climbed to the far-seeing spot from which it was possible to see down the river to the inlet.

She did not know that her great-great-grandmother had come long ago to this same spot. No one in the tribe remembered now that in the days of the great tribal conflicts, before taking his place in the war canoe each man had blown his breath into a strip of dried kelp, tied the strip into a ring, and placed the ring around the neck of his wife saying, "Guard well my breath." Keetah's great-great-grandmother had hung the ring at the head of her bed and when she had returned to the house to check it, and found the kelp ring flabby, she had come to this spot to watch for the returning canoes, to see if her husband was in his accustomed place. And she had called loudly upon all the gods, the guardian spirits of the tribe, to help her. "Come wolf, come swimmer. Come raven, come eagle"; even upon the cannibal who lived at the north end of the world.

But Keetah could not choose between Mark and Jim. She prayed for both, waiting hour after hour. When she saw the canoe enter the river and the blanket-wrapped figure who sat on the center crosspiece, she could not tell which he was, and she started back to the village, down the smooth shale, through the dark trees, the devil's club scratching at her arms.

When she entered the village, she saw the old men gathered by the ceremonial house, and as she passed them, she heard their voices.

"We must plan carefully. There is much to do."

"But the Bishop will not come for two days. This gives us time."

"Yes, but others will come with him. There will be visitors from all the villages and many guests to be housed and fed."

"We have time. The RCMP has not yet given the permit, and the boat has not yet brought the box from Alert Bay. It will be late tomorrow before they bring the body and by then all the searchers and the fishermen will be home to help us."

Keetah walked slowly to the vicarage and up the steps to the door, afraid to open it, dreading whichever truth waited her. Then she went in.

At the kitchen table sat Jim, his head buried in his arms. He lifted it slowly.

"You have been crying."

"It is the salt water that stung my eyes. I have not cried since I was eight and made a mistake in the dance, and my mother scolded me."

"You have been crying because you loved him also. What will you do now?"

"I will fish on my uncle's boat. In the fall when the fishing days are almost over, I will put up the sides and roof of my house, and in the winter I will finish the inside of the house, and I will ask you to plan it as you wish."

"And then?"

"Once I would have sent my sisters to bring you

to my house, and thus you would be my wife.
Now I will wait. When you come I will not bang
on the table when I want coffee. I will not leave
you too much alone in the village, and each year I
will take you out and show you the big world, because Mark said that when the village is gone, we
too must be able to walk across the bridge."

"When the house is ready, I will marry you."

In the evening every house in the village was
lighted and there was much talk.

"Who will dig the grave? Who will cut away
the underbrush from the path?" And the young
men answered, "We will do it."

"And who will cut the cedar for the wreaths?
Who will search the woods for the new green
ferns?" And the children answered, "We will go."

In the house of Mrs. Hudson the young matrons said to her in Kwákwala, "There will be
many guests. What meat shall we prepare for
them?"

"Roast beef."

"And how much?"

"A hundred and fifty pounds."

"And what vegetable?"

"Carrots," and tears trickled down the cheeks of
the matriarch. "He never liked mashed turnips
and I made him eat them. I am a stubborn
woman who wants her own way." And the young
matrons moved closer to her like chicks to an old
hen, "Oh, no—no—no."

By late afternoon of the next day, all was
ready. The path was cleared. The grave was dug.
The wreaths were made. The church was swept
and cleaned. The beds in the vicarage were made
up with fresh linen. The village was waiting and
listening, and it was the children who heard first

the canoes coming up the river, and they ran down the main path calling, "They come now. They bring him now."

In his tiny house the teacher heard the running footfalls on the path to the river bank, and he went quickly to the door and could not open it. To join the others was to care, and to care was to live and to suffer.

The tribe waited on the bank, and when the canoes came around the bend in the river, the old people began a chant of sorrow in the ancient language which the young no longer knew. "Aie-aie-aie—he has left us—aie-aie-aie," until even the breeze seemed to whisper it, and the trees to sigh of it.

Then the men of the tribe waded into the icy water to meet the canoes, each man taking his turn carrying the body of the young vicar to the black sands of Kingcome, while the women sang an ancient hymn to a Supreme Being whose existence had been sensed before the white man had ever come to this land. And when the body had been prepared for burial, six men carried the box into the church, the tribe waiting there. They placed it on trestles before the altar, and T. P., the elder, took his place at the lectern which was the golden eagle and spoke the Lord's Prayer, the tribe joining him:

> Kunuh Umpa Laka ike Mayauntla Hyis
> Glikum us: gak la hyis gikasa us;
> . . . .
> Au uma gagila gakunuh
> Laka yaksami.

In the night the only light in the village was that from the lantern which Jim had placed in the little church of Saint George. The village was quiet and at peace.

In her house old Marta lay awake in the dark, and she said softly, "Walk straight on, my son. Do not look back. Do not turn your head. You are going to the land of our Lord."

In the last house of the village, Peter, the carver, lay awake also, and he remembered that in the old days when a great chief died, his soul came straight back to the village in the sleek black body of a raven, and the soul of a lesser man returned in his own body no higher than an inch or as a ha-moo-moo, a butterfly. Peter did not believe this literally. Yet it seemed likely to him that the soul of the young vicar would return to the village he had loved, as would his own, and surely it would be most inhospitable if no one was awake and waiting. Thus he dressed and sat on the top step of his house in the dark night, and hearing the rustle of some small night creature he, too, spoke softly, "It is only old Peter, the carver, who waits here, friend."

Past the village flowed the river, like time, like life itself, waiting for the swimmer to come again on his way to the climax of his adventurous life, and to the end for which he had been made.

Wa Laum
(That is all)

The Laurel logo stands for the finest in contemporary fiction and nonfiction